"The guest room's yours anytime…"

"And risk getting snowed in again?" Julia shivered just thinking about it—and *not* because of the cold. Nope, it was the proximity with an all-too-attractive mountain man. "Not sure I want to chance it."

Lane shrugged. "Just offering."

Hard to believe the man used to be a lawyer. Weren't they supposed to have poker faces? Lane Bromley wore his emotions too close to the surface, and right now, disappointment was written large on his face.

The obvious signs were getting harder to ignore—he was starting to like her, too. Could this relationship get any more complicated?

Sliding behind the wheel, she said, "Keep me posted about the guardianship plan. I'll be in touch about visiting Tate this weekend."

"Just be careful." A half smile turned up one corner of his mouth. "Tate needs both his grandparents around."

Returning his smile, she began to relax. They could do this.

Whatever differences lay between them, wherever this inconvenient—and apparently mutual—attraction might lead, they could handle anything… for the sake of their precious grandson.

Award-winning author **Myra Johnson** writes emotionally gripping stories about love, life and faith. She is a two-time finalist for the ACFW Carol Award and winner of the 2005 RWA Golden Heart® Award. Married since 1972, Myra and her husband have two married daughters and seven grandchildren. She and her husband reside in Texas, sharing their home with two pampered rescue dogs.

Visit the Author Profile page at LoveInspired.com.

His Unexpected Grandchild

MYRA JOHNSON

LOVE INSPIRED
INSPIRATIONAL ROMANCE

LOVE INSPIRED®
INSPIRATIONAL ROMANCE

ISBN-13: 978-1-335-59729-8

His Unexpected Grandchild

Love Inspired
22 Adelaide St. West, 41st Floor
Toronto, Ontario M5H 4E3, Canada
www.LoveInspired.com

Printed in Lithuania

Recycling programs
for this product may
not exist in your area.

MIX
Paper | Supporting
responsible forestry
FSC® C021394

Mercy unto you, and peace, and love,
be multiplied.
—*Jude* 1:2

For Jacob and Rylee,
I never thought I'd visit Montana except in
summertime, but I wouldn't have missed your
beautiful March wedding by a frozen lake for
anything. Happy first anniversary!

And with gratitude to my friends
from CenTex Christian Writers
for your brainstorming help during
the early stages of this novel. You're the best!

Chapter One

Lane Bromley didn't like surprises. Just under two weeks ago, he'd gotten a big one, and his emotions had run the gamut: Elation. Disappointment. Resentment. Relief. Underlying them all, right down to the soles of his all-weather lace-up boots, was pure panic.

Parked outside the Frasier Veterinary Clinic on the outskirts of Missoula, Montana, he stared through the streaked windshield of his maroon 4x4 truck. He probably should have phoned first to make sure Julia Frasier, DVM, was on duty today. But then he might need to explain why he'd specifically asked for her, and since he hadn't had a pet since he was a kid... Well, that would get a little complicated.

A little? It didn't get much more complicated than having his estranged daughter show up out of the blue with a toddler in tow. Shannon was skinnier than when she'd been a lanky adolescent, and she was so depressed she could barely string three words together.

And the kid. Cute as he was, little Tate arrived looking like Shannon hadn't bathed him or put him in clean clothes for days. Beyond the dirty face, grime under his fingernails and a mild case of diaper rash, he seemed otherwise okay—and surprisingly good-natured despite it all.

I have a grandson!

Lane still hadn't gotten his head around the idea.

Just then, an SUV careened into the space beside his. The driver shoved open his door, smacking the passenger side of Lane's truck.

"Why, you—" Fuming, he got out and stormed around the tailgate to confront the offender. His mud-spattered seven-year-old truck had been through a lot worse, and showed it, but it was the principle of the thing.

"Can you help me? I've hit a dog." The man was red-faced and hyperventilating. He pressed a button on his key fob as he stumbled toward the SUV's liftgate. "I hope I got here in time."

Inside the cargo area lay a massive gray beast, blood seeping from multiple injuries. One hind leg looked mangled. The poor thing whimpered with every breath. At the sight of the suffering animal, Lane was having his own problems drawing oxygen.

He swallowed a couple of times. "I'll go find someone."

Inside, he went straight for the counter and addressed a young guy in green scrubs. "There's a badly injured dog out front. It's huge. You'll need a gurney or something."

The kid—his name badge read Dylan—looked up with a start and then raced down a hallway. Seconds later, he reappeared lugging an orange contraption with carry handles and safety straps. Two more techs followed him.

Lane held the door, pointed toward the SUV and watched from a safe distance while the techs did a quick evaluation before maneuvering the whimpering dog onto the stretcher.

Once they'd taken the animal inside, the driver turned to Lane. "The dog will be okay now, right? Because I can't wait around. I'm already late for an important job interview."

Not my problem, he wanted to say. "I'm sure they'll do what they can. But shouldn't you—"

Before he could finish, the man dived behind the steering wheel and slammed his door. Lane had barely enough presence of mind to memorize the guy's license plate as he sped away. Grumbling, he leaned inside his truck to dig out a pen and scrap of paper from the console.

As he jotted down the plate number, Dylan returned. "Sir, we need to get some information about your dog."

"It's not my dog. And the guy who brought it took off."

The tech's brows quirked. "She's his dog?"

"No, he said he hit it with his car. I have no idea whose dog it is." Lane could barely keep his frustration in check. The morning wasn't going anything like he'd planned. "Look, I just need to speak with Dr. Frasier. Dr. *Julia* Frasier," he emphasized after glancing at the three names stenciled in black and gold on the front door.

"She's taking the dog straight into surgery, so it could be a while. In the meantime, maybe you could tell us what you do know so we can try to locate the dog's owner."

Dragging a hand across his stubbly beard, Lane sighed. "Sure. Whatever."

Good thing his neighbor across the valley had been available to come over and keep an eye on Tate. The Vernons, living off-grid in the Montana mountains even longer than Lane, had raised four kids of their own, so he'd left the tot in good hands.

He hadn't intended to be gone this long, though. On his way into the clinic, he texted to make sure Lila Vernon could stay a little longer. Her thumbs-up reply and quick message to say they were doing fine relieved his mind somewhat.

That still left the problem of why he'd come looking for Julia Frasier. Before he spoke with her, he'd better have a clearer head than he did at the moment.

Behind the counter, Dylan starting typing at his computer terminal. "Your name, sir?"

"Bromley. Lane Bromley." He spelled it out.

"And the man who brought the dog—do you know his name?"

"Never saw him before, and we weren't exactly exchanging pleasantries."

The desk phone buzzed. Dylan picked it up and listened a moment. "Thanks, Amy." He hung up and typed something else into the computer. "The dog isn't microchipped, and she wasn't wearing a collar or tags. Too bad the driver didn't stick around long enough to at least tell us where the accident happened."

"I got his plates." Lane slid the scrap of paper toward the tech. "But I need that back. He did a number on my truck door."

Dylan copied the information and then returned the paper. "Help yourself to coffee while you wait."

Lane stuffed the scrap into his pocket—like he'd ever really follow through. The hassle wouldn't be worth it. He considered returning to meet Julia Frasier at a better time, but his mountain cabin outside Elk Valley was over an hour's drive northwest from Missoula. For now, at least, the winding roads to his place were clear, but who knew what tomorrow or the next day would bring? This was late August in Montana, when weather at higher elevations could change in the blink of an eye.

Ignoring the curious stares of a couple of clients waiting with their pets, he ambled over to the beverage machine. While a single-serving pod of dark roast brewed, he perused the wall decor. Something about heartworm prevention, another poster touting the value of regular checkups...

Then he came to a portrait of the Frasier family—an older couple, maybe late sixties, and an attractive fortysomething woman, all smiles and wearing white lab coats with stethoscopes looped around their necks.

He leaned in for a closer look at the younger Dr. Frasier. With her heart-shaped face and dark brown hair, there was a definite resemblance to Tate. Looked like he'd found the other half of his grandson's family.

Now the real question was, how would Julia Frasier react to learning her son was a father?

"That was a close one, Amy." Julia stuffed her surgical gown into the hamper. "She's going to be in a lot of pain when she wakes up, and I don't want that leg getting infected. Keep a close eye on her."

"I will, Dr. J."

The complicated surgery would have been even more touch-and-go without Julia's most qualified tech to assist. The dog should recover, but she'd likely end up with a limp. There'd be some disgruntled patients out front, though, since their appointments had been delayed because of the emergency. Hopefully, Julia's dad had been able to cover for her…for the time being, anyway.

Always in the back of her mind was her parents' impending retirement. They were both in their early seventies now, and over the past few months, Julia had noticed her father's gradually worsening hand tremors. He'd attempted to hide them from both Julia and her mother, but Julia had grown concerned enough that she'd begun monitoring her father's appointment schedule and tactfully stepping in for the more delicate procedures.

Julia's mother, staff veterinarian as well as office manager for over thirty years, had already cut back her hours. On top of her routine appointments, Julia had taken over most of the management responsibilities as well, and the strain was wearing. She desperately needed to hire a new office manager and bring one or two new vets on board—and soon, before she completely burned out. The plan had always been for her son, Steven, to join the practice once he completed veterinary school. But those dreams had died with him.

The phone intercom buzzed. Amy answered, and after listening a few seconds, she glanced back at Julia. "Dylan says that man is still out front waiting to speak to you."

She forced her mind to the present. "And he has no connection with our patient?"

Amy shrugged. "That's what he claims."

"Guess I'd better find out what he wants." Frowning, Julia donned a lab coat over her blue scrubs and adjusted her ponytail.

Slipping up beside Dylan at the front desk, she glanced around. A well-built man in a plaid shirt and jeans stood staring out the front window. The gray in his short, messy hair and scruffy beard gave him a rugged look.

To Dylan, she whispered, "Does our visitor have a name?"

"Lane Bromley."

Didn't ring a bell. She raised her voice. "Excuse me... Mr. Bromley?"

He turned with a start. "Dr. Julia Frasier?"

"Yes. What is it you needed to see me about?"

As he started for the counter, one of the other techs came out to call for the next patient. Julia smiled and nodded as the elderly Mrs. Gardner got up with her feisty black-and-tan min pin. Dad would have his hands full with that little guy, but at least he only needed a routine exam and annual shots.

Mrs. Gardner jerked her head toward Julia's visitor and whispered, "Watch out for him. He's a strange one."

The man's scowl suggested he'd overheard. He directed his attention to Julia. "We should talk in private."

Frowning, she showed him to her office, where his masculine presence dominated the room.

"I can only spare a moment, Mr. Bromley," she said from behind her desk. "I'm already behind with my patients."

"After what I have to say, you may want to reschedule those appointments."

Her brows shot up. "I'm not sure I care for the tone of this conversation. Maybe you should just come out with it."

"You should sit down."

More than a little unnerved, she could only hope he wasn't about to slap the office with a veterinary malpractice suit. Had her father's tremors caused a problem when she hadn't been on hand to intervene? If only she or Mom could convince Dad to get a checkup.

She lowered herself into her chair, fingers tightening around the armrests. "All right, I'm sitting."

He sat across from her and suddenly didn't look so imposing. Rather, he looked…scared. "Sorry, this isn't easy." He hesitated, his gaze drifting to something behind her on the filing credenza. "Is that your son?"

She didn't have to turn around to know he was looking at one of her last photos of Steven. Her heart squeezed. "Yes," she murmured, lips tight. "He… He passed away two years ago."

"I know."

Her chin shot up. "Who exactly are you, and how do you know my son?"

"I never met your son. I wish I had. Maybe then…" His Adam's apple worked. He looked away.

The suggestion that Bromley's business here had something to do with Steven unsettled her even more. "Would you please get to the point?"

He pulled a cell phone from his shirt pocket. After tapping some icons and scrolling a few times, he slid the phone across the desk. "It's about him."

Her roiling stomach warned her not to touch his phone, much less look at whatever he wanted to show her. Hands still locked on the armrests, she shifted her glance to the phone screen.

Her breath hitched. *Steven?*

She glared at her visitor. "Where did you get a baby picture of my son?"

"That little boy isn't your son. I only snapped this three days ago."

"Then who—" One hand flew to her mouth, as if she could stifle the realization. This couldn't be Steven's child. He would never have kept anything like this from her. They'd always talked about everything. *Everything...*

Really, Julia?

True, they hadn't communicated as often after Steven started college. During his last few months, she'd sensed him holding back about something and had assumed he'd taken the hint that the topic of his rekindled faith in God was off-limits with her.

But a baby? Never in a million years.

Clamping down on a pang of guilt, she swiveled in her chair and gathered the photo of grown-up Steven to her chest. "You'd better start at the beginning."

Bromley gave a weak laugh. "This is almost as new to me as it is to you. I only found out about Tate—that's his name—less than two weeks ago."

Sinking deeper into his chair, he rested his hands on his thighs and looked toward the window. In a quiet voice, he told her how his daughter, Shannon, whom he hadn't seen and had rarely heard from since she left for college five years ago, had shown up unannounced with her nineteen-month-old son. All he could get out of her was that she couldn't cope anymore, that she only wanted to curl up and die—but she couldn't let herself until she knew Tate would be taken care of.

"After she came home," he went on, "I didn't dare leave her alone for a minute for fear she'd harm herself. A friend helped me get her admitted to a mental health facility."

"I'm so sorry." Julia felt for the man, but she had other issues. "You still haven't explained how you determined Tate is…is Steven's."

"I found a marriage certificate among Shannon's things." He produced the document, spread it open in front of her, and indicated the couple's printed names and the signatures beneath them: Shannon Elise Bromley. Steven Edward Halsey.

Julia's heart spasmed. It was unquestionably her son's unique scrawl. "Halsey was my ex-husband's last name," she murmured. Then she read the wedding date. "They were married almost *three years ago*?"

He cast her a thoughtful stare. "You really didn't know."

She briskly shook her head while a thousand different explanations paraded through her mind. Not a single one of them jibed with the person she'd thought her son to be. "Go on," she said stiffly.

"Obviously, I wanted to know who he was and why he'd deserted his wife and child. So I did some digging and learned he'd been a student at Washington State, and that he'd been killed in a motorcycle accident. His obituary made no mention of Shannon, so I assumed it was because his family hadn't approved of their marriage. But seeing your face just now, I realize…" His expression softened. "Doing the math, I figure your son died a few months before Tate was born."

Again, she couldn't speak.

"I get that this is a huge shock for you," the man said. "I know it was for me."

"My son had a wife. A baby!" A sob stole its way into her throat. "Why didn't he tell me?"

"I can't answer that. I still have a lot of questions myself." Bromley fished something else from his pocket. "I did find this among Shannon's things." He extended his closed fist and dropped a ring in the center of her desk.

She immediately recognized the exquisite antique—the scrolled rose-gold band, the emerald-cut amethyst bearing an intaglio rose of Sharon, a tiny diamond marking its center. Heaving a shaky sigh, she picked up the ring.

"It was passed down from my great-grandmother. When Steven was home on a school break a year or so before he died, he asked to see it. I didn't know he'd kept it."

"I thought it must be an heirloom. I'm guessing it was meant to be Shannon's engagement or wedding ring, but I don't think she'd been wearing it, so if you want it back…"

Pressing the ring to her heart, she pictured her son, how preoccupied he'd seemed in the last year of his life. When he'd stopped coming home as often, she'd wondered if he'd met someone. In fact, she'd cautioned him about not allowing anything to interfere with his studies.

Was that why he'd kept his marriage a secret?

Hurt and bewildered, she placed the ring on Bromley's side of the desk. "Your daughter is my son's widow and the mother of my grandchild. The ring belongs to her."

"That's kind of you. I'll keep it safe until she's better." Pocketing the ring, he stood and roughly cleared his throat. "I know this has taken you by surprise, but after you've had time to process it all, I hope we can come to an understanding about Tate's immediate future."

Her eyes snapped open. "*Understanding?* You show up out of the blue and drop this bombshell on me, and I'm supposed to somehow *process* it so *we* can make decisions about a grandson I never even knew existed?"

"Sorry, guess that sounded a little too…expedient." Releasing a groan, he raked his fingers through his hair. "I wasn't sure how this meeting would go, and I'm still figuring out how to deal with everything."

Julia paused for a bolstering breath. "You're right. We do

need to consider the practicalities. But first, I want to meet my grandson and my—" she choked down the lump in her throat "—my son's widow."

He nodded. "They aren't letting Shannon have visitors yet, but you can come out to my place to meet Tate. Under the circumstances, I'm trying to keep things as stable for him as I can."

"Of course." She mentally reviewed her schedule—not that she wouldn't turn the world upside down for this chance. "I could come tomorrow. When would be a good time?"

"Whatever works for you." He retrieved his phone. "Give me your number and I'll text you directions."

Anticipation building, Julia provided her personal cell phone number. "Is there anything Tate needs? Clothes, toys, other supplies?"

"Shannon didn't bring much, so I've been working through a list. My next priority is a crib and bedding, which I'm planning to pick up while I'm in town today."

"I've kept Steven's crib in storage all these years, hoping someday…" She pressed her trembling lips together.

The man offered an understanding smile. "That would really help, if you're sure you're okay with it."

"Certainly. We can—"

A knock interrupted them, and Amy peeked in. "Excuse me, Dr. J, but…um…your father may need assistance with a patient."

Working closely with Julia's dad, the tech had actually been the first to notice his tremors. Ever since, she'd been helping Julia keep an eye on him.

"I'll be right there." When the door closed again, she turned to Mr. Bromley. "I need to get back to work. We can talk more tomorrow, though. And I'll bring the crib."

"That'd be great, Dr. Frasier. Thanks."

"All things considered, I think we can dispense with formalities. You can call me Julia."

"Julia." He dipped his chin. "In that case, I'm Lane."

"Tomorrow, then…Lane. I'll text when I'm on my way."

Showing him out through the reception area, she fought to corral her scattered emotions. Since long before Steven's death, professional detachment had become her shield. After what she'd just learned about her son on top of everything else weighing her down, she needed that self-control now more than ever.

But once 6:00 p.m. rolled around and she left the clinic behind, she intended to pull out her favorite photos of Steven and indulge in a good, long, purging cry.

Summer days in Montana were long, but once the sun slid behind the mountains, darkness descended quickly. It was after eight thirty by the time Lane finished his errands in town and made it home, so he'd needed his headlights to see the winding gravel road—more to make sure he didn't hit an elk or bear than to show the way. After twenty-plus years living off-grid and turning this remote patch of land into something he could call home, he knew the road's every twist and turn.

He left the engine running while he got out to swing open the wide tubular ranch gate, then closed it again after he'd driven through. Easing past Lila's Jeep, he parked in the carport beneath the cabin. After a quick detour to the barn and chicken house to tend his livestock, he trudged up rough-hewn log steps to the deck and let himself in the front door.

Beneath the yellow-white glow of a reading lamp, Lila looked up from the book in her lap. "You told her?"

"I did." His neighbor knew why he'd made the trip into Missoula. "She's coming out tomorrow to meet him. And bringing a crib—her late son's."

"Oh, that's sweet…and sad." She closed her book and stood. "You must be hungry. I've got some ham-and-bean soup on the stove."

He followed her to the kitchen but wasn't sure he could scrape up an appetite. "Is the baby asleep?"

"Mmm-hmm. That little guy's good as gold. Such a little trouper." She paused to face him, her silver-streaked auburn braid falling across one shoulder. "You've got to make a plan, though, Lane. You know I'll come over to help whenever I can, but with winter right around the corner, we're busier than ever these days."

"I know, I know." Living off the grid meant taking advantage of every warm day to prepare and stock up for next winter. Bleary-eyed, he made his way to the table. Shortly, a steaming bowl of soup appeared in front of him. "Thanks, Lila. You're a good friend. You and Dan both."

"Hah. Ever since we sold you this property, we've been just about your *only* friends. And that's not good, either. You've spent too many years alone in these mountains, Lane. You know good and well it's why Shannon left home in the first place."

He was too tired to argue. Besides, she was right. "It's getting late. You should head home. And watch out for bears."

She harrumphed. "Bears around these parts know better than to mess with me." Shoving her arms into a nubby cardigan, she backed toward the door. "Holler if you need anything. And you might try praying, too."

Pray? Like that would ever happen. "Good night, Lila, and thanks again."

"The train's comin' into the station, so open wide!" Lane made a train-whistle sound as he aimed the spoonful of oatmeal at Tate's mouth.

Balanced on Lane's knee, the little boy spread his lips just enough while eyeing his grandpa as if he'd come from another planet.

He sighed and spooned up another bite. "Sorry, kiddo, my toddler-feeding skills are pretty rusty."

"Mama?" Tate pointed toward the back door.

"Mama's not better yet. I promise we'll visit her as soon as the doctor says it's okay. Now eat your breakfast so you can grow up big and strong."

Across the table, Lane's cell phone chimed. His cabin was barely within range of the nearest cell tower, but with a signal booster, texts usually went through. He handed Tate the spoon. "Here, you try while I see what that's about."

It was a message from Julia Frasier. Just leaving storage unit with crib. Didn't realize you lived so far into the mountains. Should I bring bear spray? Emergency rations? Personal locator beacon?

So the veterinarian had a sense of humor. With Tate dribbling more oatmeal onto Lane's jeans than he managed to swallow, he texted back: Ha. Ha. Gate will be open. Drive on through to the cabin. See you in about an hour, give or take.

More like an hour and a half, considering Julia didn't know the mountain roads like Lane did. He should probably meet her where the Vernons' drive branched off in case she got confused.

Once he got both himself and his grandson cleaned up, he decided he ought to straighten up a bit. While Tate sat on the floor stacking handmade wooden blocks—the same ones Lane had shaped and sanded more than two decades ago for Shannon's enjoyment—he whisked a feather duster over every flat surface, straightened the stack of books by his easy chair, tidied the kitchen and put out clean hand towels in the downstairs bathroom.

Next, he needed to run down and open the gate. With Tate bundled into a lightweight hoodie and pint-size lace-up hiking boots, they began the slow trek down the driveway. Lane was just unlatching the gate when he glimpsed a lime-green

Toyota 4Runner rounding the bend. Anyone could see that thing coming a mile away. Recognizing Julia Frasier behind the wheel, he waved and motioned her through.

A short way past him, she pulled to the side and cut the engine. Gaze fixed on Tate, she slowly stepped from the vehicle. She looked much different today in a long-sleeved crimson top and skinny jeans. Her dark brown hair was tucked behind one ear and grazed her shoulders. The overall effect was softer, somehow. More approachable. More real.

"Hi, little guy." Her voice was high-pitched and shaky. "I'm your... I'm..." Taking quick breaths, she seemed unable to finish the statement.

Lane scooped Tate into his arms. "Maybe we should go on to the house."

She nodded, then got back into her vehicle and followed him as he marched ahead. He stood at the base of the steps and pretended not to notice while she sat in the car for a moment to blow her nose.

"Down," Tate insisted, leaning over so far that Lane was afraid he'd fall on his head.

"Easy there." He righted him and gently set him on the ground as Julia emerged from her car.

Kneeling with one hand beckoning Tate, she could no longer hide the tears she obviously hadn't wanted Lane to see.

After a glance up at him, the toddler slowly went to her. He pressed her cheeks between his hands. "No cwy. It be otay."

Now the floodgates opened for real, and Lane's heart twisted to witness Julia's raw emotion as she enfolded their grandson in her arms.

How quickly this little boy must have had to grow up over the past few months if he'd already learned how to comfort a woman in tears.

Shannon, how could you do this to your own son?

Chapter Two

❧

"Go Mama now?" Tate pointed past Julia's shoulder toward her SUV.

Confused, she looked up at Lane, who quietly shook his head. Stroking the little boy's cheek, she said, "No, honey, I'm sorry."

Tate stamped his foot. "Go Mama now!"

"Tate, that's enough." Lane swooped up the little boy and tucked him against his hip. "Let's go inside."

Pulling herself together, Julia followed them upstairs to the deck and entered a rustic but well-appointed living room— paneled walls, wood floors, a woven earth-tone area rug, plush leather sofa and chairs. Across the room, another flight of split-log stairs rose to the second story, probably to the bedrooms. Dying embers glowed behind the glass door of a wood-burning stove, a reminder of how much chillier it could get up here in the mountains, even in August. Thankfully, the stove had been babyproofed with a makeshift barrier.

Tate refused to be held a moment longer. "Go Mama!"

Lane had barely set him down when the quick little guy darted past Julia toward the front door.

Picturing him tumbling down the outer stairs, she spun around. "Tate, no!" As he tried to work the door latch, she captured his pudgy fingers. "No, honey, you can't go out there."

Lane caught up and threw a bolt on the upper part of the door. "He won't be able to get it open now."

Fighting to slow her breathing, she stood shakily and swiped at another escaping tear. Her thoughts seesawed between past and present. One moment, she saw this adorable little boy she'd only just met, and the next, her mind was racing back through time to when she'd realized what a mistake she and her then-husband had made letting their ground-level apartment go and moving with fourteen-month-old Steven into a two-story town house.

She felt a tug on her jeans. "It otay now," the boy murmured. "It be otay."

This wasn't right. One hand on her stomach, she cast Lane a troubled frown.

"I know," he murmured. "He kept comforting Shannon like that. She couldn't seem to stop crying."

"It's good you got her into treatment. But what about Tate? Has he seen a doctor yet?"

"It's one more thing on my long and growing to-do list." Grimacing, he sank onto the ottoman in front of an easy chair. "I am so far out of my depth here."

"Clearly." Spying a plush toy on the sofa, Julia used it to distract Tate. "What are you thinking, trying to take care of a toddler up here in the middle of nowhere? This place doesn't even register on my GPS."

"Which is why I gave you explicit directions." Lane glared. "And what gives you the right to start passing judgment on a situation you only walked into five minutes ago?"

"How quickly we forget." It took all her self-control to keep from raising her voice above a whisper-shout. "You *pulled* me into this so-called *situation* when you came to my clinic yesterday. And anyway, when it comes to my grandson, I have as much right as anyone to pass judgment."

"Our."

"What?"

"Tate is *our* grandson."

Momentarily taken aback, she sucked in a breath. "Fine. *Our* grandson needs to be somewhere a lot safer than a remote mountaintop." Chewing her lip, she pondered the options. Now that her mother was semiretired and more available to help, surely Julia could do this. "I think you should let me take him."

"What? No way!" He pushed to his feet, seized her by the elbow and dragged her past the stairs and into the kitchen. "Shannon is Tate's mother and my daughter, so I'll be the one making decisions about his care."

"But didn't you come looking for me so *we* could—I think your exact words were—*come to an understanding* about our grandson's future?"

"Which does *not* mean letting you rip him out of my arms to go live in the wild and dangerous big city." He emphasized the last part of his statement by clawing the air like an angry bear.

She huffed and crossed her arms. "What do you have against the city, anyway, Mr. Mountain Man?"

The wounded look that came into his eyes drove home how very little she knew about Lane Bromley. It also made her wish she could snatch back the last few minutes of this increasingly heated exchange and start over. They were both too emotionally wrecked for anything resembling a rational discussion.

Taking a beat to reassess, she glanced around the kitchen. She was almost surprised to find he had all the modern conveniences—gas range, French-door refrigerator, microwave. Granite countertops, ceramic tile floor, a brass chandelier resembling elk antlers that looked like a smaller version of the one she'd noticed in the living room. For a mountain man, he appeared to live pretty well.

Even so, he was miles from what she considered civilization. Miles from medical help should Tate become ill or fall down the stairs or burn himself on the stove…

Spying a coffeemaker with an almost-full carafe sitting on the warmer, she tipped her head. "Is that fresh?"

Lane blinked as if mentally returning from another time and place. "As of an hour ago."

"May I?"

He gestured toward a cupboard. "Clean mugs are in there. If you want cream, be warned. It's fresh from the source."

So he had a milk cow. Figured. However, she preferred her dairy products pasteurized. "Black is fine." An almost empty mug embossed with a bison head sat next to the coffeemaker. "This must be yours. Want a refill?"

He glanced toward where they'd left Tate playing in the living room before turning back with a sigh. "Sure. Thanks."

At least they'd returned to polite civility instead of attacking each other. Perhaps now they could make real progress.

After setting his mug on an oblong wood-grain table, she pulled out a padded chair at the opposite end. The set looked custom-made. Waiting for Lane to join her, she took a careful sip and let the coffee's calming warmth seep into her chest.

"This is good," she said. "Dark and full-flavored, the way I like it."

Retrieving his mug, he shifted a chair sideways and sat so he could keep an eye on Tate. His tender devotion to his grandson touched her, but his obstinacy ignited a bonfire of buried resentment. Just like Julia's ex, Lane Bromley needed to face reality and do the right thing for his family.

"Look, I get it. I can't take care of Tate like I should without help. But for reasons I won't get into, I don't care much for the trappings of city life."

His eyes darkened in that haunted expression again. Something traumatic must have triggered his flight to this mountain refuge. Perhaps it had to do with Shannon's conspicuously absent mother? Probably not a good time to bring it up, though.

Instead, she said softly, "I think we both want what's best for Tate. For starters, he should be seen by a pediatrician. Would you trust me to get some recommendations?"

He stared into his coffee mug for so long that she wasn't sure he'd registered the question.

Before she could prompt him to answer her, Tate toddled into the kitchen and raised his arms to Lane.

"Ho' me."

Wordlessly, the man set aside his mug and drew the little boy onto his lap. Julia suppressed a stab of envy—not that she had any right. Tate had spent the last several days getting comfortable with his grandfather. Still, she ached to hold her grandson again.

With Tate nestled under his whiskery chin, Lane glanced toward her and drew a long, slow breath. "Okay, yes, whatever you can find out."

Julia swallowed her emotions along with a quick sip of coffee. "I'll make some calls as soon as I get back to town."

"But Tate stays with me," Lane added with a pointed look. "That's nonnegotiable."

And just when she'd thought they were making headway. *One battle at a time*, she told herself. Eventually, though, she intended to make the obstinate man see things her way.

Did she really believe he hadn't noticed the smug twist of her lips? If the woman thought she could change his mind about keeping Tate, she had another think coming. "You said you brought the crib. Maybe we should get it set up."

Her smugness morphed into barely disguised annoyance. She rose stiffly. "I'll keep an eye on Tate while you bring it in."

"It's close to his mealtime, if you want to feed him. He has a thing for tortillas and hummus with turkey slices. It's all in the fridge. There's apple juice, too."

"Good, I was hoping you knew better than to give him raw cow's milk."

"I'm not totally incompetent." Casting her a withering look, Lane set Tate in the chair he'd just vacated and scooted him up to the table. "Gramps'll be right back, okay? Sit here while this nice lady fixes you some lunch."

"The nice lady has a name, *Gramps*," Julia said with fake levity. "Tate, can you say Grammy?"

"Gammy, Gampy." The little boy pointed to each of them in turn. Then he tapped his own chest. "I Tate."

The kid was a prodigy. Lane couldn't help but grin.

On his way through the living room, his smile faded as he glimpsed a photo collage of Shannon through her childhood years. How had his little girl grown up so fast…and drifted so far away?

Shannon had been around Tate's age when he'd brought her to the mountain to start anew after her mom had been snatched from their lives.

Tessa had been a part-time paralegal at a small downtown law firm where Lane had been an associate. One night, she'd returned to the office after hours to grab a file he'd forgotten. Worried when she'd taken longer than expected, he'd asked a neighbor to watch Shannon while he went looking for her. He'd found the office door ajar and his wife bleeding from a gunshot wound to the chest. By the time an ambulance arrived and rushed her to the hospital, she'd lost too much blood. She died two hours later on the operating table. The police surmised she'd come upon a burglar looking for drug money, but an arrest was never made. For months after, Lane had ping-ponged between helpless rage and unrelenting guilt.

And Julia wondered why he despised the city.

Shaking his head to clear away the memories, he marched out to Julia's SUV. It took three trips to haul in all the crib parts. If any nuts or bolts were missing, he could probably find substitutes in his well-stocked workshop. He'd expanded it over time, right along with his carpentry and mechanical skills—absolute necessities for living off-grid. He also made a modest income from the handcrafted wood furniture he'd developed a knack for creating. He could never thank Dan and Lila Vernon enough for taking him under their wing all those years ago—not to mention how they'd helped him get his bearings as a single father.

After piling crib parts inside the door, he went looking for Julia and Tate. They sat kitty-corner from each other at the kitchen table, and it looked like Julia was wearing most of Tate's lunch.

Using a wet dishcloth to wipe hummus out of her eye, she scowled at Lane. "You could have warned me."

"Why?" He suppressed a snicker. "Seeing you like this is way more fun."

Tate's gleeful cackle wasn't so polite. "Gammy messy!"

"She certainly is, and so are you, little guy." Lane hefted him out of the chair and held him at arm's length. "I'll take him upstairs to clean up. You can use the downstairs bathroom."

After scraping lunch remains off his grandson and dressing him in a fresh pair of dungarees, he figured Julia might appreciate a change of clothes as well. He selected a maroon sweatshirt from his closet, carried it and Tate downstairs, and tapped on the bathroom door. "I'm hanging a clean shirt on the doorknob for you. We'll be in the living room figuring out the crib."

A few minutes later, she appeared wearing the sweatshirt over jeans that showed a few damp areas from spot cleaning. She extended her arms, and the sleeves of his shirt drooped past her fingertips. "It's a little big, but thank you."

Standing there wearing his shirt, her face washed clean of makeup and her hair swooped into a messy topknot, she looked ten years younger and not nearly so antagonistic. A knot formed in his belly. It wasn't exactly unpleasant, but it was definitely disconcerting.

He cleared his throat and forced his attention back to the crib. "Did you bring directions for this thing?"

She crossed to the chair where she'd set down her purse and returned with a yellowed sheet of paper. "Here you go."

He gave a low whistle. "I'm impressed you still had it after all these years."

"I never throw away anything important. I'm extremely organized."

He might use a slightly different term for that level of efficiency, but he'd keep it to himself. "If I'd had more time, I could have built a bed for Tate."

She stroked the curved back of a wooden rocking chair. "You made this, didn't you? And the table and chairs in the kitchen."

"I did." Woodworking had given him a renewed sense of purpose, something immediate and tangible he could do to ward off the guilt and grief.

Arching a brow, she nodded. "And now I'm duly impressed."

"Aren't we just the mutual admiration society?" He sank back on his boot heels. "So. Are you planning to stand there and supervise, or are you willing to pitch in and help me put this crib together?"

Julia wasn't sure whether he'd meant his remark in jest or as a not-so-subtle criticism. Frowning, she folded her arms. "You should figure out where you're going to put the crib before you get much further."

"Good point. I'm such a sound sleeper that I don't think I'd hear him in Shannon's old room. There's plenty of space in my room, though."

"Where has he been sleeping?"

"In bed with me." Lane snorted. "Which hasn't exactly been conducive to a good night's rest."

Remembering how squirmy Steven was when he used to crawl in bed with her, Julia gave a snicker. "Then let's move it before it gets any more unwieldy. And you should invest in a good baby monitor, too."

"I picked one up while I was in town yesterday."

While Julia kept Tate occupied stacking wooden blocks, Lane hauled everything upstairs. Joining him, she found his bedroom to be airy and spacious with a beamed wood ceiling and an expansive view of the forested valley behind the cabin. In truth, *nothing* about this place—other than the rustic-chic decor and the fact that the house was actually made of logs— fit her definition of *cabin*.

With a little help from Julia to hold the various sections in place, Lane soon had the crib assembled. He moved it near a window and, on Julia's advice, shortened the venetian blind cord so Tate couldn't reach it. She'd resigned herself to leaving the little guy with Lane for now, but once she had a better handle on her work and personal life, she'd pressure him into letting her take over their grandson's care.

A peek out the window told her the afternoon was wearing on. And were those snow flurries in the air? "Looks like the weather's changing. I should leave soon."

Together, they stretched a crib pad and fitted sheet over the mattress. In the meantime, Tate had filled his diaper, so she helped Lane change him. Oh, the memories!

Once they'd finished, she decided to get on the road. Downstairs, Lane handed her a canvas shopping bag for the top she'd tried to rinse out in the bathroom sink. "Thanks for bringing the crib. I'm sure Tate and I will both sleep a lot better tonight."

"I didn't save too many of Steven's baby things, but if I come across anything else useful, Tate's welcome to use it." She slid her arm through her purse strap. She hadn't thought to bring a jacket, but Lane's thick sweatshirt should keep her warm until she got home. "I have to be in the clinic all day tomorrow and until noon on Saturday, but if you get desperate for help—"

He scoffed. "Too late for that."

"Just saying." She knelt and held out her arms to Tate. "Got a goodbye hug for Grammy?"

He poked out his lower lip. "Go bye-bye?"

"Yes, but I'll see you again soon." And for keeps, if she had anything to say about it—at least until Shannon recovered. "You take care of Gramps till then. Promise?"

Giving a firm nod, he stepped into her embrace. It was all she could do to tamp down another spate of tears as she gave him a kiss on the cheek. She stood brusquely while she retained any measure of control.

Lane hefted Tate and pulled open the front door. "Uh-oh. I don't suppose you've switched to snow tires yet?"

Her stomach sank. "It's only August. I hadn't expected to need them already."

"Well, you may be staying the night. It's coming down pretty hard."

She pushed past him to see for herself. He was right. The scattered flurries she'd glimpsed from the upstairs window had thickened into a swirling white curtain. She could barely make out the shape of her vehicle, much less Lane's gate or the road beyond. But this was Montana. Why should she be surprised by a freak August snowstorm?

While her brain raced with all the reasons she absolutely could not get stranded up here, her phone chime signaled an incoming text. Backing away from the door, she fished her phone from her purse.

The message was from Amy: Our hit-and-run patient is

running a fever. Leg looks infected. May need more surgery. When will you be back?

One hand to her forehead, she paced to the window. Maybe it wasn't snowing *that* heavily...

"Bad news?" Lane asked.

If anything, the snow was coming down even harder. Julia forced down a swallow. "The dog you brought in yesterday. She's taken a turn for the worse."

"It wasn't me who brought her in, remember?"

"Whatever." She wasn't going to let the poor girl lose a leg if there was any way to save it. "I really have to get out of here."

He set Tate down and heaved an apologetic shrug. "Unless you want to risk sliding off the side of the mountain, I'm afraid you're stuck here."

A long, frustrated groan rumbled in her throat. Each of her patients earned a special place in her heart, but for some reason, it was even more true with this one. It couldn't be because the huge gray dog happened to arrive the same morning Julia learned she was a grandmother.

Her mother's surgical skills weren't as sharp as they used to be, but the thought of her father stepping in if the dog did require another operation... She couldn't take the chance. Maybe she could talk Amy through the procedure, or else have her transport the dog to the veterinary emergency center.

Lane gently took her arm. "You look like you need to sit down."

What she needed was to find a way down this mountain, but apparently, that wasn't happening.

As she sank onto the nearest chair, Tate toddled over and patted her knee. "Gammy sad?"

His tender concern squeezed her heart. "Grammy's worried about a sick doggy."

At the word *doggy*, Tate's eyes lit up. "Gammy have doggies?"

"Yes, I have two little doggies who live with me. Their names are Daisy and Dash." She pulled Tate onto her lap, his sudden interest in dogs a welcome, if temporary, distraction. "Grammy is a doggy doctor. Do you know what a doctor is?"

He gave a firm nod. "Make Mama all better. Go see Mama now?"

Well, she'd opened up that can of worms. She looked to Lane for help.

He knelt next to the little boy and tugged on his shirttail. "Hey, Tater Tot, looks like Grammy's staying for supper. You can help me figure out what to fix, okay?"

While Lane took Tate to the kitchen, Julia considered how to reply to Amy. She hadn't yet told her parents or anyone else about Tate or mentioned where she'd be today. She couldn't, not until she'd confirmed in her own mind that she hadn't dreamed up a grandson or anything else Lane had told her yesterday in her office. A text seemed a cumbersome way to try to convey the gist of the situation, but with barely one bar showing on her phone screen, she didn't have much choice.

Snowed in at a friend's place in the mountains. Phone service horrible. Increase antibiotics & call Dr. Martinez at vet ER if she continues to worsen. Keep me posted.

Amy would understand why she didn't want her father involved. Hopefully, he'd already gone home for the day and wouldn't take it upon himself to intervene. Next, she sent a similarly vague text to her mom and asked her to take care of Daisy and Dash until she could get back to town.

A savory aroma wafting from the kitchen evoked a growl from Julia's stomach. Since she was stranded here, she may as well make herself useful. With a sigh, she pushed to her feet. "Anything I can do to help?"

Lane couldn't remember the last time he'd had an actual dinner guest—much less one who'd be staying overnight. Why hadn't he been paying closer attention to the sky? If he'd taken note of the weather change even an hour earlier, he could have sent Julia on her way and spared himself the awkwardness.

"I hope spaghetti's okay," he said as she joined him in the kitchen. "You could set the table."

"Happy to." Moving toward the cupboard he indicated, she stepped around Tate.

Wielding a wooden spoon, the kid pretended to stir something in a dented metal bowl. He looked up with a mile-wide grin. "I cook."

Hard as it was keeping up with a toddler, the little guy was shining a light into crevices of Lane's heart that had too long persisted in darkness.

Julia carried plates to the table. "That sauce smells delicious."

"It's my special recipe, made from homegrown tomatoes and herbs. Can't claim credit for the pasta, though. My friend Lila makes it from scratch and always sends over a batch."

An arched brow was Julia's only response. He hoped it meant she was revising her opinion of him as an uncouth mountain man.

When the food was ready, Julia filled water glasses while he prepared a small bowl of spaghetti and sauce for Tate.

She frowned as he cut the pasta into spoon-size pieces. "I think you'd better take charge of feeding him tonight—unless you want marinara stains all over the shirt you let me borrow."

He shot her a pointed look. "So he's *my* grandson when you'd rather not get messy?"

"That isn't what I meant." Returning his stare, she set the water glasses at their places and took her seat.

With Tate situated on a chair close enough for Lane to assist as necessary, he scooted up to the table and spread a cloth napkin across his lap. "I'm not religious, but feel free to say grace if you're so inclined."

She fidgeted with her napkin. "I'm not on speaking terms with God, myself."

There was obviously some hidden pain there, not surprising after the death of a son. Lane had lost his faith—what little he'd had—when Tessa died. "Okay, then. Dig in."

An uncomfortable silence descended as they ate, interrupted only when Lane had to stop Tate from slinging spoonfuls of marinara-drenched spaghetti. Afterward, Julia offered to clean up the kitchen while Lane took the boy upstairs for a bath. He wasn't sure who got the worst end of the deal.

With his sweet-scented little grandson wearing footed brushed-flannel jammies, he carried him downstairs and turned him over to Julia in the rocking chair. After stoking the woodstove for the night, he donned jacket and gloves and trudged out to tend his livestock. By the time he returned, Tate had fallen asleep in Julia's arms, and she looked about ready to nod off as well.

Seeing them like that, both looking so peaceful, brought an ache to his chest. All these years, he'd refused to admit how lonely he really was. Now he knew he never wanted to feel that way again.

Chapter Three

Lane awakened the next morning to the yowls of a hungry toddler. "Out! Me out!" the kid yelled as he shook the crib rails. "Hung'y!"

"All right, I'm coming." Lane stumbled out of bed, surprised he'd slept so soundly. The past several days must be catching up with him. Not to mention for the first night in two weeks, he hadn't been continually hammered by a little boy's nocturnal karate chops.

Beyond the window, morning sun reflected off a fresh layer of snow—close to ten inches, judging from what Lane could see of the fence line. Julia wouldn't be getting out of here any time soon.

Propping the kid on his hip, he tiptoed out. No sound yet from the bedroom across the hall. He went downstairs to get some coffee brewing and to start a batch of scrambled eggs. With one eye on Tate, he stirred the eggs while scrolling through a series of text messages from neighbors asking if he could help clear roads. From early fall through late spring, his truck's snowplow attachment got plenty of use, and normally he wouldn't hesitate. But now he had Tate to consider, and he couldn't be in two places at once.

Although if Julia woke up soon, she'd probably be glad to watch Tate if it meant she could be on her way sooner. The lady vet might be bossy and opinionated, but he'd seen the look in her eyes as she'd read the text about the injured dog. It was like saving the animal's life truly mattered to her.

That was the problem, though. When anything—people, pets, possessions—began to matter too much, things got risky. People died or moved on. Animals, too. Possessions wore out or got stolen. Lane had learned the hard way that the less he cared, the less he got hurt.

Yet here he was setting himself up to be hurt again. He was already getting too attached to the little guy playing bongos on the bottom of an old saucepan.

As he sat sharing a plate of eggs with Tate, Julia wandered in. The coffeemaker drew her like a magnet, and she didn't speak a word until she'd poured herself a mug and taken several tentative sips. Then, as if noticing Lane for the first time, she offered a raspy "Good morning."

"To you, too." He caught himself staring at how unaffectedly pretty she looked with uncombed hair and wearing his raggedy plaid flannel robe over her clothes from yesterday. Clearing his throat, he poked another spoonful of eggs into Tate's mouth. "Soon as this little guy finishes, I'll scramble another batch. I can fry up some sausage, too."

"Coffee's all I need. I don't usually eat breakfast." She plopped down at the opposite end of the table. "When will they get around to plowing the roads up here?"

He snorted a laugh. "*They* equates to *me* and a couple of my neighbors. These roads aren't maintained by the county."

"Oh. I didn't think about that." She darted a worried glance toward the window. "But I *have* to be at the clinic this morning."

"Did you hear more about the dog?"

"My senior tech texted a few minutes ago. Last night I had her adjust antibiotics, and she says the swelling is down this morning, so it looks like the leg—" She rolled her eyes. "Sorry, get me talking about my patients and I'll bore you to death."

"It's okay. I can tell you're concerned."

"I am. But not just about the dog." Eyes closed briefly, she gave her head a quick shake. "It's…been a difficult couple of years."

She looked and sounded like a woman who sorely needed to get something off her chest. He wasn't sure he wanted to ask, but he couldn't help himself. "If you feel like venting, you've got a captive audience."

Her dismissive laugh wasn't convincing, especially when the next sound was a choked-off sob. "Steven's death hit me hard." She stood and paced to the window over the sink, as if giving him her back would make it easier to keep talking. "He was smart, gifted, genuine—and so tenderhearted. He would have made a wonderful veterinarian."

Tate had finished eating, and Lane dabbed a smear of egg off the boy's chin. "I didn't realize your son was studying to become a vet."

"He would have joined the family practice after passing his licensing exams. Ever since he first expressed interest as a teenager, I dreamed he'd someday be working alongside me."

Lane knew about broken dreams. "I'm sorry."

Julia refilled her mug and drifted back to the table. "I don't know what I'm going to do now. My mother has already cut her hours in half, and my dad…" Her jaw clenched. "He won't admit it, but he needs to retire."

"Why? Is something wrong?"

"He's developed a hand tremor. He hides it well, but it's getting worse."

Again, he murmured, "I'm sorry."

"So to keep the practice going, I need to recruit one or two new veterinarians, plus hire an office manager." She looked toward the window. "I had a very promising interview scheduled for ten o'clock this morning, and now I'm going to miss it."

Frowning, Tate patted Lane's wrist. "Gammy sad. Make Gammy all better?"

Giving the kid a gentle hug, he smiled at Julia. "I'm afraid I can't fix all Grammy's problems, but I'll see what I can do about clearing the road."

Less than three hours later, Julia was on her way down the mountain. She wouldn't make the interview appointment as scheduled, but the candidate had kindly agreed to come at one o'clock instead.

The hardest part was leaving Tate. Having spent the past twenty-four hours at Lane's place and seeing how conscientiously he cared for the little boy, she had slightly fewer qualms about their grandson's well-being. However, she still believed she was better equipped to be Tate's guardian while his mother underwent treatment. If today's interview went well, she could be that much closer to freeing up the time she'd need.

She made a quick trip home to change clothes—Daisy and Dash would have to stay at Mom's for a few more hours—then hurried to the clinic. The first hour was spent helping to clear the morning's patient backlog. That kept her too busy to answer questions about where she'd gone yesterday and why. There'd be time for explanations later.

Once the waiting room had emptied, she checked on her hit-and-run surgical patient. Amy was in the back tending to another canine patient, and when Julia reached the big girl's kennel, she found a new label on the door.

Head tilted, she turned to the vet tech. "Rowena?"

"It fits, don't you think? I looked it up online, and it can mean 'joy' or 'white mane.'" Amy knelt and scratched the dog's nose through the wire mesh. "She definitely has a white mane, and this pretty girl needs all the joy in life she can get."

"I agree. Bring her out so I can take a closer look at that leg."

The huge dog patiently endured the examination, even licking Julia's chin despite the discomfort she must be suffering. Julia guessed the mostly gray dog to be part Great Dane, part Irish wolfhound, with possibly another large breed or two mixed in. Tipping the scales at nearly 125 pounds, the dog appeared to be between two and four years old.

"Has Dylan had any success tracking down an owner?"

"Nothing," Amy replied. "He did find out where the accident happened, but no one in the neighborhood remembers seeing the dog around there before."

More than likely, someone had fallen in love with her as a puppy, then soon realized they couldn't afford the food bill for a dog that size and turned her out. The mere thought of such irresponsibility made Julia shudder.

"What are we going to do with her, Dr. J?"

"If no one claims her by the time she's ready to be released, I'll ask Maddie if she has space in her kennel, at least for a short-term stay while we find other arrangements." Julia's best friend, Maddie McNeill—Maddie Wittenbauer since her marriage earlier this year—owned and operated Eventide Dog Sanctuary, a loving "forever" home for senior and otherwise unadoptable dogs.

"Rowena's too sweet to end up at a shelter," Amy said with a pout. "You know how hard it is to find good homes for big dogs like her, which means…"

Julia knew exactly the outcome Amy couldn't bring herself to speak of. "We're not there yet." She gave Rowena a gentle neck massage. "Let's keep asking around, and have Dylan post her photo on our Facebook page."

"She should have a home outside the city with lots of acreage," Amy mused. "A family with kids. She seems like she'd be great with little ones."

Memories evoked a bittersweet smile. After the divorce, Julia and Steven had moved into a house with a big backyard where she still lived. Shortly afterward, they'd adopted Buff, a ninety-pound yellow Lab mix who'd become her son's best pal. Happy little boys and big, tail-wagging dogs…it was a combination that never failed to swell her heart.

Then a new image formed—a giggling Tate clinging to Rowena's shaggy fur as they trotted across the meadow that was Lane's front yard. Oddly, she could picture herself there, too, sharing the moment with Lane…laughing together, holding hands…

She clamped her teeth together. Clearly, she was more emotionally and physically wrung out than she'd realized. After giving Amy further instructions for the dog's care, she escaped to her office. Hopefully, a protein bar and mug of strong coffee would sustain her through the one-o'clock interview.

After Friday's disappointing meeting with a veterinarian who'd blatantly padded his résumé, then an office manager applicant canceling at the last minute on Saturday, Julia felt like she was starting over from square one. Maybe she needed to adjust the job descriptions she'd posted on the employment search websites.

On Monday morning, she drove out to Eventide Dog Sanctuary, where she routinely provided discounted veterinary services to the twenty-plus canines in Maddie's care. Once the dogs were attended to, she asked if Maddie had time to talk.

"Sure. Come to the house and I'll put the kettle on—

unless you require the super-caffeinated dark roast you usually drink."

"Actually, a cup of your calming lemon-ginger tea might be in order."

Stepping into the mudroom, Maddie looked back with an arched brow. "This sounds serious."

"Like a heart attack." Julia collapsed into a kitchen chair while her strawberry blonde friend boiled water and set out mugs and tea bags.

A few minutes later, their tea steeping, Maddie sat across from Julia. "All right, what's going on?"

Where to begin? Maybe just blurt it out? "I have a grandson."

"You...*what*?" Her friend looked almost as stunned as she'd been when Lane had first passed the photo of Tate across her desk.

"It's true." Tears formed against her will. "Steven got married without telling me. His son was born a few months after he died." Haltingly, she described her first encounter with Lane, then the trip up the mountain, getting snowed in and the precious hours spent with her little grandson. "Tate looks so much like Steven that I'm on a continual seesaw between past and present."

"A grandson... I'm speechless." Maddie squeezed her hand. "Do your parents know?"

"I broke the news over the weekend. They're thrilled about having a great-grandchild, of course. But Dad thinks I should hire a lawyer to make sure my rights are protected."

"Is that really necessary at this point?"

Julia dunked her tea bag a few times. "I'd say no, except for the fact that Lane is adamant about being the one to care for Tate. I'm trying to convince him otherwise, but he's this tough off-gridder mountain man, who for unknown reasons has serious issues with anything city-related."

Maddie scoffed. "When Witt first came into my life, I distinctly remember you pestering me about doing a thorough background check."

"Advice you ignored at first."

"Because he'd given me no reason not to trust him. However, in your case, there's a child involved, and while taking legal steps might be premature, you deserve to know a few more details about Tate's other grandparent."

"I don't disagree."

After a thoughtful sip from her mug, Maddie asked, "Is there a Mrs. Bromley?"

"Not as far as I can tell. Lane's place is homey, but I got no sense of a woman's touch anywhere."

"And Tate's mother—you said she's in a mental facility?"

"Lane had her admitted to Mercy Cottage."

"I've heard good things about it. I'll be praying they can help her."

Maddie's faith had grown in leaps and bounds since she'd met Witt. Julia wasn't sure what it would take for her to let God back in. She gulped the last of her tea and stood. "I almost forgot. Do you have space in the kennel for my recovering hit-and-run victim?"

"I wish I could help, but tomorrow I'm taking in two more senior dogs with health problems, so I'm about to be full up again."

"I understand. I'll figure out something." If all else failed, she could keep the dog at her house temporarily—which would mean a huge adjustment for her spoiled-rotten twin dachshunds. "Let me know when your new arrivals are settled, and I'll come check them over."

When Julia returned to the clinic, she recognized Lane's

mud-encrusted dark red truck parked out front. Oh, no. Had something happened to Tate?

She drove around to the rear parking area, rushed inside and halted at her open office door. Lane sat facing the opposite wall, one knee jumping nervously.

Heart pounding, she barged in. "Where's Tate? Is he all right?"

He stood abruptly. "He's okay. He's with my neighbor."

"Then what are you doing here?"

"I just came from Mercy Cottage. Shannon had—I forget what the doctor called it—some kind of episode." He collapsed into the chair and pressed his palms against his eyes. "She isn't going to get well any time soon."

"Lane, I'm so sorry." Julia hung her shoulder bag on the rack next to her lab coat, then closed the door and took the chair next to his. "Can I do anything?"

"No," he said, massaging his temples. "I just… I couldn't think straight after leaving there."

He was clearly terrified for his daughter. She lightly touched his shoulder. "At least she's in a safe place and getting care."

The intercom on her desk phone buzzed. Her mother's voice came over the speaker. "Julia? I thought I heard you come in. Your dad could use some help in exam room two."

Lane stood abruptly and pulled in a noisy breath. "You're busy. Anyway, this isn't your problem. I'll go."

"Lane, wait." She stayed his hand as he reached for the doorknob. "Shannon was my son's wife. She's Tate's mother. I care very much what happens to her."

"I appreciate that, but still… I shouldn't have bothered you. We'll be fine."

"Fine?" The word grated on her. "There's nothing *fine* about this, and certainly not for an innocent little boy whose mother is so depressed she wants to die."

"It was a rhetorical *fine*, okay? Tate's not fine. I'm not fine." Exhaling tiredly, he looked toward the ceiling. "None of us are fine."

His vulnerability threatened to undermine her self-control. Arms folded tightly against her ribs, she murmured, "I do need to get to work, but keep me posted about Shannon. I'll visit Tate again as soon as I can break away. Or you can bring him here. Just let me know."

He replied with a noncommittal grunt and strode out without looking back.

Endearingly unguarded one minute, obstinate and unreadable the next—the man was an enigma. And Julia didn't like puzzles. Life was supposed to make sense.

Hers hadn't since Steven died, no matter how hard she worked at making it so. Especially now, with a grandson who'd quickly stolen her heart, plus the growing urgency to restaff the clinic before her mother fully retired and her father could no longer safely practice.

No, she definitely did not need the added complication of totally unbidden feelings for Lane Bromley.

Going straight to Julia's office after his visit to Mercy Cottage? What had he been thinking? Lane hated feeling so inadequate. So powerless. So…bereft.

What he *really* hated was this sudden atypical impulse to turn to a relative stranger for help. Let alone a smart, savvy and—yes—beautiful woman like Julia Frasier. He had enough on his plate worrying about his daughter and getting over the shock of becoming a grandfather. Finding himself thinking of Julia in terms of anything other than Tate's other grandparent was both inconvenient and unnerving. Since losing Tessa, he hadn't so much as considered letting someone new into his life. Hadn't wanted to. Hadn't needed to. And the fact that these feelings were coming out of nowhere *now* threw him even more off-balance than he already was.

Best to keep his focus where it should be—on looking after his grandson and making sure his daughter got better. He could only hope he hadn't made a huge mistake by entrusting Shannon's treatment to the medical system he'd lost all confidence in the day Tessa died.

On the positive side, he was figuring out all over again how to be sole caregiver for a toddler. Dan and Lila's two eldest daughters used to help watch Shannon when she was little, but the Vernon kids were all adults now with families of their own, and he'd already imposed quite a bit on Lila these past several days.

Over the weekend, though, he'd designed and constructed a portable play yard that he could set up near wherever his chores took him. Tate was already getting a kick out of watching his grandpa milk the cow and tend the chickens, and yesterday afternoon, he'd busied himself "planting" with a trowel and pail of garden soil while Lane worked in the greenhouse.

The memory brought a smile to Lane's lips. It also reminded him he was running low on homogenized milk and a few other food items the picky toddler would eat. Heading home through Elk Valley, he swerved in at the mini mall and parked in front of the grocery mart. The place was never busy. All the same, Lane didn't relish these trips to town, whether it was bustling Missoula or tiny Elk Valley, which was little more than a wide place in the road.

Inside, he grabbed a carry basket and headed straight to the dairy section. He added milk, yogurt and sliced cheese to the basket, then he browsed the breakfast cereal row. Shannon had brought along some sugary brand that couldn't possibly be healthy, but Tate wasn't fond of Lane's hearty steel-cut oatmeal—neither the texture nor the prep time.

As he perused the ingredients list on a box of organic cereal, a woman with a reddish-blond ponytail reached for a box on a nearby shelf. Looking over at him, she smiled. "These labels can be so confusing."

Lane snorted. "Tell me about it. And the picture looks like birdseed. How do I know if my kid will even eat it?"

"How old?"

"Almost twenty months." When the woman's brows lifted ever so slightly, he added, "My grandson. I'm keeping him for a while." He turned away, hoping she'd take the hint.

He could feel her gaze on the back of his neck. Lowering her voice, she said, "Forgive me for making assumptions, but... would he be Julia Frasier's grandchild, too?"

His shoulders tensed. Small towns—go figure. "If you're asking me that, then you already know the answer." He glared over his shoulder. "As I'm sure half of Elk Valley does by now."

Stepping closer, she lowered her voice. "Julia is my best friend, and she confided in me. Naturally, I'm concerned. And, well, you fit her description of a...a..." Color crept up her cheeks.

He faced her squarely. "What? A misanthropic mountain man?"

A guy around Lane's age sauntered up behind the woman. He cast Lane a wary glance before asking, "Everything okay, honey?"

"Just comparing notes on breakfast cereal." With a stiff smile that reminded Lane of his no-nonsense fourth-grade teacher, she offered him the box she'd been holding. "Here, try this one. It's a favorite of ours."

"Th-thanks." Now he was embarrassed for overreacting. He'd descended the mountain more times in the last two weeks than he sometimes did in an entire year, and his people skills showed it.

A soft bark alerted him to the scruffy black-and-tan dog pressed against the man's knee. Taken aback at first, Lane noted the red emotional support animal vest.

"Easy, Ranger," the man said as he offered Lane his hand. "I'm Witt. This is my wife, Maddie. Haven't seen you around before. Are you new in town?"

Apparently, the man wasn't privy to whatever Julia had told his wife. "Not exactly." Lane hesitantly accepted Witt's handshake. "Lane Bromley. I live up the mountain."

"Nice to meet you. And don't mind Ranger. Everyone around here knows we're a package deal, but Maddie thought he should start wearing the vest so we get fewer strange looks." Witt gave the dog a scratch behind the ears. "He's saved my life more than once. Well, him and my amazing wife," he added, tucking the woman under his arm.

Love filled her eyes as she smiled at her husband. It was the same look Lane used to see every time Tessa cast a smile his way. Would he ever stop missing her? "Well, I… I need to get going."

Before he could duck past the couple and their dog, Witt halted him, a knowing look shadowing his deep-set eyes. "Hang on a sec." He took a business card and a pen from his pocket. After jotting something on the back of the card, he handed it to Lane. "This may sound a little weird, but I feel like the Lord's telling me you could use a friend. Here's my cell phone number. Call me anytime."

Lane could only nod as he accepted the card and continued toward the cashier. He didn't doubt he'd been giving off a few too many "disgruntled loner" vibes, but no way was he buying into the idea that God had anything to do with the man's offer.

Either way, it didn't matter. Lane wasn't the type to have heart-to-hearts with guy friends. Bad enough he'd bared his emotions a few too many times already with Julia. What was it about her that brought out his vulnerable side?

Whatever it was, he'd better put a lock on it before this breach in his defenses opened any wider.

Chapter Four

❧

It was finally the weekend again, and Lane expected Julia any minute. Tied up at the vet clinic all week, she hadn't been able to break away for another trip up the mountain. After Lane had seen her on Monday, she'd texted with a pediatrician recommendation and then followed up often to ask how their grandson was doing. She'd repeatedly asked for photos and videos, but with his spotty cell service, transmitting files that size was next to impossible.

Once she got here, maybe she wouldn't mind watching Tate for a few hours. This time of year, he usually made his last few trips into the forest in search of fallen or standing dead trees to top off his firewood supply for the winter. After three weeks of nearly full-time toddler duty, a solo excursion into the peaceful Lolo National Forest was sounding better all the time.

Mind? Julia would probably shove him out the door and then lock it behind him.

He and Tate had just finished lunch when he glimpsed her lime-green SUV come through the gate.

"Grammy's here." He propped the tot on his hip and strode out to the deck. As last week's snow melted away, the first days of September had turned pleasantly balmy—no need for anything warmer than a flannel shirt over a long-sleeved tee.

"There's my sweet boy!" Julia scurried up the steps and

held out her arms for Tate. "I've missed you so much. Have you been good for Gramps?"

Hooking one arm tightly around Lane's neck, the kid gave his head a firm shake. "I want Mama."

Julia's pursed lips betrayed her disappointment.

"I told you, Tater Tot," Lane said. "Mommy's very sick. She'll be home when she's better." He tamped down a twinge of self-satisfaction over the boy's attachment to him. "But Grammy's come all this way to see you, and she looks like she really needs a hug."

After a thoughtful pause, Tate leaned toward Julia. Snuggling him under her chin, she cast Lane a grateful smile.

A few minutes later, she sat cross-legged on the living room floor and helped Tate stack blocks. Keeping her voice low, she asked, "What's the latest on Shannon? Any improvement?"

"Yesterday, they let me speak with her on the phone for a few minutes." Lane sank onto the ottoman, memories of the call making his stomach knot. "She sounded so…out of it. The doctor said the meds can do that while she adjusts, but I don't like it."

"I'm sure they know what they're doing. Give it time."

The doctors know what they're doing, Mr. Bromley. Yep, he'd heard that before. And then his wife had died in surgery.

He rose abruptly. "Can I leave you two alone for a while? There's stuff I need to do while I've got someone to keep an eye on Tate."

"Please, do whatever you need to. In fact…" Uncurling her legs, she pushed to her feet. "Would you consider letting Tate come home with me for a couple of days? I imagine you have plenty of jobs around here that would be much easier to manage without a toddler underfoot."

He didn't care for her ingratiating smile, but he couldn't exactly deny the logic of her suggestion. "All his things are here." His reasoning was weak, but it was the best he could come up with.

"So pack him a bag."

"What about his crib?"

"My neighbor has a portable crib I can borrow."

"He can be a picky eater."

"Then make me a list. There's a supermarket just up the road from my place."

Fists jammed against his hips, he forced himself to take a breath. *I need him here*, he wanted to insist. *With me. Where I can be absolutely certain he's safe.*

Except there were no guarantees, were there? He'd tried to keep Shannon safe, and look how she'd ended up.

He exhaled loudly. "Just drop it, okay? We can talk when I get back."

A tug on his pants leg drew his attention. Tate's tiny hand gripped Lane's jeans, while the other clung to the hem of Julia's plaid overshirt. He frowned at each of them in turn. "Gammy, Gampy, no fight. Gammy, Gampy, be nice."

Snickering, Julia shot Lane a wink. "Guess he told us."

Lane stooped to lift the little guy into his arms. "We aren't fighting, Tater Tot." *Not exactly, anyway.* "The thing is, Grammy and Gramps both love you very much, which makes it hard sometimes to agree on what's best for you."

Julia edged close enough to smile at Tate around Lane's shoulder, and a not-exactly-unpleasant ripple snaked up his spine.

"That's right," she said. "But Grammy doesn't live close by, so I'm hoping Gramps will let you come visit me at my house sometimes. Besides, your great-grandparents can't wait to meet you."

Tate drew his caterpillar brows together. "Gate-gamps?"

"Yes!" The brightness in Julia's voice matched her expression. "My mommy and daddy are your great-gramps and great-grammy."

"No need to confuse him." Lane put some space between them, more for his sake than for Tate's.

"What's confusing about letting our grandson know he has extended family?" Julia's smile didn't change, and neither did her tone, but the look in her eyes certainly did. "That he has *lots* of people who love and care about him?"

"Just…never mind. I need to head out." He lowered Tate to the floor, then knelt and tweaked his chin. "Gramps has some stuff to do, so I'm going to leave you with Grammy for a bit. That okay with you?"

Lips skewed, Tate nodded. "Dat otay."

Before Julia Frasier disconcerted him more than she already had, he grabbed his jacket, baseball cap and truck keys, and bolted from the cabin.

With his firewood permit in the glove compartment and his chain saw in the back, he didn't let himself think too much as he chose his route into Lolo National Forest. But when he spied a fallen tree conveniently near the road and prepared to haul out his equipment, the truth hit him like a rockslide: *yeah, you're lonely, but face it, that's no one's fault but yours.*

True, solitary life had become as natural to him as breathing. An only child, he'd been born late in his parents' lives. They'd been private people, too, and both had passed on before he finished law school. As for Tessa's parents, they'd never forgiven him for moving to the mountains with Shannon. They were gone now, as well, which he should be sad about for Shannon's sake—they'd maintained a relationship with their granddaughter as best they could—but he couldn't even imagine the scolding he'd get if they'd lived to see Shannon in her current state.

He deserved a big chunk of the blame, but everything he'd

done, every choice he'd made since Tessa died, had all been for his daughter.

Who are you kidding, Bromley? You turned tail and ran—and not just to protect Shannon. Truth is, you couldn't face continuing alone in the life you'd dreamed about and planned with Tessa.

After her messy first experience giving Tate lunch, Julia took precautions this time. Finding cotton dish towels in a kitchen drawer, she used one on Tate as a bib and covered her shirt with another. The toddler really needed a high chair or booster seat, but after Steven had outgrown his, she hadn't kept them. She'd definitely need to invest in some new gear before bringing Tate home to live with her.

Assuming she could convince Lane to part with him. So far, she'd made no progress in that area. One thing was clear—the harder she pushed, the more he dug in his heels. If she looked up *stubborn* in the dictionary, she'd find a picture of Lane Bromley.

No sooner had she cleaned up Tate after lunch than his head started bobbing. She swept him into her arms and started for the stairs. "Time for a nap, little man."

"No. Wock me." He pointed over her shoulder toward the rocking chair.

Within five minutes, the boy had melted against her in sound sleep, his warmth seeping into her shoulder. Memories of rocking Steven just this way brought a lump to her throat. After losing her son so tragically, she'd assumed the joy of holding a grandchild was lost to her forever, which made these moments a pure gift.

It was tempting to cuddle and rock her precious grandson until he awoke from his nap, but when her arm supporting him began to stiffen, she reluctantly carried him upstairs. As she laid him in his crib, he roused only long enough to tuck a flop-eared terry-cloth bunny beneath his arm.

She could stand there all day watching the rise and fall of his tummy and how his lips and eyelids twitched with whatever little boys dreamed about, but at last, she tore herself away. An odd feeling washed over her as she glanced around Lane's room. Though she'd helped him put the crib together in this very room just over a week ago, today it felt as if she were trespassing.

And yet she couldn't suppress her curiosity. Turning slowly, she let her gaze skim the walls and furniture surfaces. The plain decor and casually haphazard array on the bureau definitely said a single guy lived here. A mystery novel and a puzzle book lay on the nightstand, along with books on various aspects of off-grid living—greenhouse gardening, canning and preserving produce, solar power maintenance, emergency first aid...

Tucked behind the bedside lamp, as if he'd wanted to keep it near at hand but not *too* near, sat a framed photo of an attractive fair-haired woman. Seated behind a desk, she appeared to be laughing at the photographer—and not merely with amusement, but with genuine love in her eyes. The old-style bulky computer monitor on her left confirmed the photo wasn't recent.

Shannon's mother?

Lane's wife?

Swamped at the clinic all week, she'd put off delving into the man's background. Maybe it was time she followed up.

After another peek at Tate, she slipped downstairs and pulled out her cell phone. Attempts to use the internet browser quickly proved futile, so she texted Maddie and asked if she had time to search for anything connected with Lane Bromley. Moments later, Maddie replied with a thumbs-up, and then Julia paced from window to window while she waited. Hopefully, whatever Lane had gone off to do this afternoon would keep him busy for a while.

Almost half an hour went by before Maddie replied. As a part-time English tutor, she had access to newspaper archives and had come across an obituary for Tessa Bromley, survived by her husband and their infant daughter. More research had turned up a report about the law office robbery and the shooting that had ended Tessa's life.

Knuckles pressed to her lips, Julia squeezed her eyes shut. She could begin to understand now why the man had fled to this mountaintop refuge. He'd needed to grieve and to heal. Even more importantly, to create a sheltered place where his little girl could grow up in safety.

What he'd failed to account for was the cost of prioritizing Shannon's physical safety over her mental and emotional well-being. Had he fully realized it yet, or, if given the chance, would he repeat those mistakes with his grandson?

Julia absolutely could not let that happen.

After Tate's nap and a snack of dried apple slices, Julia laced up the boy's tiny hiking boots and zipped him into a hoodie. The shadows were already lengthening, but there was still a broad sunny patch in Lane's front yard. Once again, Julia imagined the little guy toddling through the grass alongside Rowena. She really must talk to Lane about bringing the dog up here, if only to foster until a good home could be found.

"Go see cow." Tate pulled her toward the barn.

"Um, I don't know about that, sweetie." Large-animal medicine had been a facet of Julia's veterinary school curriculum, and she occasionally treated Maddie's horses for their most basic needs. Cows, on the other hand? Not her cup of java.

After another surprisingly strong tug on her arm from such

a little boy, she reluctantly followed. Before they reached the barn, the sound of tires on gravel drew her attention to the road, where Lane's truck had stopped on the other side of the gate. Getting out to open it, he saw Julia and waved.

"Gampy back!" Tate would have run straight toward the truck if Julia hadn't had firm hold of his hand.

At least she'd been spared a visit with the cow. "Let's wait here for Gramps, okay?"

As Lane drove past, she glimpsed a load of logs in the truck bed. He pulled up beside a long, open-sided firewood shed that looked nearly full. Dropping the tailgate, he called, "Are you okay watching Tate while I unload this wood?"

"I think I can manage." What did the man think she'd been doing all afternoon?

Tate pointed. "Help Gampy?"

"No, honey, we'd just be in the way." Certainly Lane didn't need more evidence of the folly of attempting to raise a toddler under such demanding circumstances. Keeping a safe distance, she asked nonchalantly, "How old was Shannon when you moved up here?"

Muscles bulging as he hefted a log, he glanced from her to their grandson. "A little younger than Tate, I guess." He swung around and dropped the log onto the growing pile next to the woodshed. "And I know what you're thinking. I managed then, I'll manage now."

Not without a lot of help, she wanted to say, but bit her tongue.

She was soon entranced by Lane's rhythmic workflow as he emptied the truck bed. Each log had to weigh between seventy and a hundred pounds, yet he maneuvered them with practiced ease. Barely breathing hard, he paused only now and then to press his damp forehead against his shirtsleeve.

Realizing her heart was beating faster, she inhaled a deep

breath of her own. No matter how strong or good-looking he may be, no matter how tragic the loss of his wife had been, no matter how tenderhearted he seemed toward his daughter and grandson, she must *not* let Lane Bromley get under her skin. Tate's future depended on it.

He could feel her watching him. Judging him. Plotting how she'd convince him to let her take Tate.

He slung the last log onto the pile and latched the tailgate. Tucking his leather gloves into a pocket, he discreetly rolled his aching shoulders. This particular job got harder every year, but his only backup heat source was propane, and if he ran low, delivery could get dicey once the winter snows set in.

Julia cast a pointed glance at his store of logs. "Cutting all that wood must take a huge chunk of your time."

Her implication was clear. "I team up with Dan Vernon and another neighbor or two to fill all our sheds." With a point of his own to drive home, he continued, "I'd even venture to say that all my daily chores combined don't take near as much time as what you put in at your thriving vet clinic."

Her tight frown said he'd hit the intended nerve.

"If you're done here, I should probably be going."

"Wait." Feeling bad about needling her, he narrowed the space between them. Besides, for Tate's sake if nothing else, they needed to find a way to get along. "As late as it is, you might as well stay for supper." He scooped Tate into his arms. "How does grilled elk steaks and baked potatoes sound?"

She slacked her jaw. "I... I don't know if that's such a good idea."

"What? The steaks or the potatoes?"

"No, I meant—"

Tate giggled and stretched to touch the toe of his boot. "Tate toes!"

That elicited a laugh from Julia, and the tension between them dissipated.

"So." Lane hiked a brow. "Will you join us?"

She returned his smile with a thoughtful one of her own. "I suppose it would be okay. Now that I've been here a couple of times, I'm not as worried about getting lost going home."

Just then, the slanting sun lit a spark in her brown eyes, and Lane worried he was in danger of getting lost. He drew a quick breath. "Guess I should get cooking."

An hour later, he served up two perfectly grilled elk steaks along with bacon-seasoned green beans and tender baked potatoes topped with home-churned butter. Elk would be a little tough for Tate's tiny teeth, so Lane substituted strips of grilled chicken breast for him.

"This is all delicious," Julia said after a few bites. "Did you grow the vegetables yourself?"

"The beans are from this summer's crop. I grow potatoes in the greenhouse year-round."

She contemplated a morsel of steak. "And the elk… I suppose you're a hunter."

He glanced up. "Does that bother you?"

"I get that it's a food source, and hunting is necessary for population control." She laid her fork aside to take a sip of water. "I just couldn't do it myself."

"I didn't grow up in a hunting family. It was something I had to learn and get used to. Same as…" He cleared his throat meaningfully while pointing at the chicken on Tate's plate.

Her eyes widened. "You mean—"

"Where do you think your store-bought chicken comes from? I can assure you, my methods are a lot more humane."

"Yes, I… I'm sure the chicken had a very happy life, right up until…" Stabbing a green bean, she muttered, "I knew I should have become a vegetarian."

He stifled a chuckle. "If you can't finish your steak, I'm happy to help."

"That's okay." She sawed off another forkful of meat. "I shall somehow force myself to enjoy every last bite."

Which she did, to Lane's great amusement. While he cleaned up the kitchen, Julia took Tate upstairs for a bath and a bedtime story. When he heard her returning footsteps, he poured two mugs of fresh decaf and met her at the bottom of the steps.

Accepting the mug, she inhaled the aroma and released a blissful sigh. "You've discovered my greatest weakness."

Oddly, that pleased him. He motioned toward the sofa and then took the easy chair across from her and propped one foot on the ottoman. "Did the little guy go to sleep okay?"

"One story and he was out like a light." She sipped her coffee. "Actually, now that we have a chance to talk, I've been meaning to run an idea by you."

More pressure to let her take Tate? He wouldn't make it easy for her. Back stiffening, he set aside his mug and silently waited.

Looking a little less sure of herself, she sat forward and placed her mug on the coffee table. "You remember the injured dog that arrived at the clinic the same time as you?"

Not the direction he'd expected the conversation to take. "Hard to forget."

"Well, as quickly as she's healing, she'll be ready to leave the clinic soon."

"That's good...isn't it?" Where was she going with this?

"Yes, but we still haven't tracked down her owner, and she's too sweet to end up at a shelter. So I thought..." Her gaze became imploring. "You have such a great place here, and lots of room for a big dog to run—"

"Hold on." He lowered his boot to the floor. "You want *me* to take the dog? After you've been not-so-subtly hinting at how I've already got too much on my plate to take care of my grandson?"

"Our."

How like her to throw the word back in his face. He met her saccharine smile with a glare. "Yes, *our* grandson. Which is another reason I can't believe you're suggesting this. That dog's the size of a pony. She could hurt— Oh, wait. I get it now. You want to trade the dog for Tate."

"No!" Eyes closed, she inhaled slowly through her nose. When she lifted her gaze again, whatever subterfuge he'd imagined had vanished, replaced by a wistful melancholy. "It's just that I remember how much Steven loved the dog he grew up with. They were such great pals, and I..." The slightest tremor entered her tone. "I'd love for Tate to have that kind of special companionship."

An unexpected rush of sympathy—the only feeling he'd admit to—propelled him to the sofa. Easing down beside her, he slid his arm around her to pat her shoulder. "It's okay, Julia. It'll be okay."

She cocked her head, a quirky grin skewing one side of her mouth. "Learn that from Tate?"

He snickered. "Sometimes I think that kid is smarter than both of us put together."

"You'll get no argument from me."

"At last," he said, rolling his eyes, "one thing we can agree on."

"In addition to what's best for Tate." She shifted to face him, and his arm fell away. "So how about if I bring her tomorrow for a trial visit? We can see how the two of them get along."

"I don't know..." He already missed the brush of her silky dark hair across the back of his hand. "I was thinking I'd call Mercy Cottage tomorrow and ask if Shannon's doctor would okay an in-person visit."

"Perfect. If they won't let you bring Tate yet, you can leave him with me. Afterward, I'll follow you home with Rowena."

He narrowed one eye. "Rowena?"

"My tech gave her the name. Pretentious, I know, but it fits her regal stature."

Was he really letting her talk him into this? He stood before she weakened his resolve any further. "Okay, but just so you understand, I'm not committing to anything."

She seemed satisfied with that—*seemed* being the operative word. After finishing her decaf, she thanked him for supper and said her goodbyes.

Closing the gate behind her as she drove away, he realized he'd been so distracted by her presence that he'd neglected his evening barn chores. After checking on Tate with the baby monitor receiver he carried in his pocket, he trekked to the barn.

He most certainly didn't need another animal to feed and clean up after. He'd let Julia bring the dog for the afternoon if she must, but no way was he letting it stay.

Chapter Five

Babysitting Tate on Sunday morning gave Julia the opportunity to introduce him to her parents. They came straight over as soon as their church service ended, and to Julia's great relief, the excitement of meeting Tate effectively sidetracked them from their usual subtle hints about getting her back to church.

Once Tate understood these were the great-grandparents Julia had told him about, he ran to them for a hug. "Gate-gamps! Gate-gammy!"

Eyes filling with tears, Mom glanced up at Julia. "He looks so much like…"

"I know." Julia sniffed back a tear of her own.

Her father settled into a chair and pulled Tate onto his lap. "When you first told us Steven had a son, I had my doubts. I don't anymore."

All too soon, Lane returned from seeing Shannon. He was polite enough but seemed on edge as Julia introduced him to her parents.

Her father didn't make it any easier. "Julia says you live off-grid up in the mountains. That can't be the safest environment for a toddler."

Lane stiffened. "We're managing just fine."

"You should see Lane's place," Julia said brightly. "He's made it into a very comfortable home."

He looked surprised that she'd defended him. She'd surprised herself as well.

"Gampy." Tate grabbed Lane's hand and tugged. "See doggies."

At his questioning glance, Julia murmured, "My dachshunds. He's been playing with them in the backyard."

The little boy wasn't to be deterred, so they all filed outside. Observing Tate's fun with the frisky twins boded well for when he'd meet Rowena later. Julia only hoped the big dog's size wouldn't be too overwhelming.

More worrisome was the fact that Julia's two little dogs seemed to so thoroughly intimidate Lane. He gave them each a nervous pat, then straightened and crossed his arms. "We need to be going soon, Tater Tot."

Already? She'd find it a lot harder to let them leave if they hadn't already confirmed plans for her to come up to the cabin today…unless Lane had changed his mind. "We're still on for this afternoon, right?"

"Give me an hour or so. I need some time."

For what, she couldn't imagine, unless he'd had a difficult visit with Shannon. Later, she'd ask him how it went.

As soon as Lane drove away, Julia's mother cornered her in the entryway. "Honey, that little boy is as precious as he can be, and I understand why you want him here with you until his mother gets well. But how do you propose to manage the clinic *and* raise a child? Not that I won't help as much as I can, but—" Glancing into the den to where Julia's father had tuned to a football game on TV, she lowered her voice. "I know you've been covering for your dad's tremors. Once he admits it's time to retire, I'm afraid I'll have more than I can handle just taking care of him."

It was the truth, though not what Julia wanted to hear. "I know, Mom. I'll figure out something. In the meantime, Tate's doing okay with Lane, and I'm going up to check on them as often as I can."

"And the interviews?" Her mother worried her lower lip. "Julia, we have to make some decisions soon."

"I spoke with a couple of promising candidates last week." She grimaced. "But Dad insists on having the final say, and he's been digging in his heels."

Mom squeezed Julia's hand. "You pick the people *you* want to work with. Let me deal with your dad."

"Thanks, Mom." She gave her mother a hug. "I know this isn't easy for you, either. I promise I'll do everything possible to make sure Frasier Veterinary Clinic continues to thrive."

It was just after two thirty that afternoon when Julia parked in front of Lane's cabin. She made sure she had her cell phone ready to video Tate's reaction when he met Rowena for the first time.

"Gammy back!" Tate called as Lane walked him down from the deck.

She smiled and waved. "Yes, and Grammy's got a big surprise for you, sweetie."

Leaning into the back seat, she clipped a leash on Rowena's collar and guided the dog to the ground. Fresh from the bath and toenail clip Dylan had given her yesterday, the gray canine with white mane looked every bit as regal as her name implied. The blue cast on her hind leg would remain for another month or so, but the dog had adapted well. Her superficial injuries had almost fully healed.

Camera at the ready, Julia moved to the side so Tate could get his first glimpse of Rowena. His wide-eyed gasp of delight didn't disappoint.

"Gampy!" he shouted, bouncing on his toes. "Dat my pony?"

"No, Tater Tot," Lane said, his expression skeptical, "that's just a great big hairy dog."

Julia walked the dog closer. "She's a lot bigger than Daisy and Dash, but she's very friendly. Her name's Rowena. Want to pet her?"

"Hey, careful." Lane positioned himself between Tate and the dog.

But Tate had a mind of his own. "Moo, Gampy." He shoved at Lane's knee. "I pet Weena."

"Slowly, though," Julia cautioned. "Remember how I showed you how to say hi to Daisy and Dash the first time?" She knelt and stretched out her arm, palm down, fist lightly closed. "Hold your hand like this and let her sniff it."

Rewarded with a wet tongue across his knuckles, Tate pulled back with a giggle and then tentatively extended his hand again. This time, Rowena nosed his pudgy fingers open and offered her head for a pat.

Tate's look of exquisite joy swelled Julia's heart. Her thoughts flashed back to Steven's first encounter with Buff as a squirming puppy, and for a moment, she couldn't breathe.

"Here, let me," Lane said softly, taking her phone. "I'll get some shots of all three of you."

"Oh. Thanks." She'd almost forgotten the video camera was running. There'd probably be several shaky frames of sky and earth.

Dabbing her damp cheeks with her sweater sleeve, she laughed with Tate as Rowena patiently accepted his clumsy pats and unintentionally vigorous tugs on her fur. Soon, he asked for the leash so he could walk Rowena himself. When he took over like a pro, and the dog obediently followed, Julia thought her heart would burst.

Giving a loud sniffle, she stood. "What did I tell you? They're going to be besties forever."

He snorted and returned her phone. "I don't even know how to take care of a dog."

"What? You never had one growing up?" She noticed the video was still recording and pushed the stop button.

"My mother had a froufrou lapdog that had to go to the groomer once a month. She came home with hair ribbons and painted toenails and smelling like a cross between roses and flea dip. The critter never did like me, and I still have scars to prove it."

"Oh, Lane." Julia stifled a chuckle, now understanding his discomfort around the dachshunds. On impulse, she snapped a photo of his grumpy expression.

"Hey, delete that." He grabbed for her phone.

"No way." She danced out of reach. "That shot needs to go in Tate's baby book."

His brow furrowed. "I don't even know if he has one."

"Shannon didn't start one for him?"

"If she did, it wasn't with her stuff."

Considering what the young mother had gone through, losing her husband, raising their baby alone, Julia suspected Shannon hadn't had the emotional energy to even think about a baby book. In that case, Julia would take on the project, both to capture Tate's childhood years and as a tribute to Steven.

The thought brought a resurgence of her own grief. She clamped down hard to keep her chin from trembling. *I miss you so much, Steven. I wish you could see this little boy of yours.*

Tate was walking Rowena in a small circle in front of them. When he stumbled, Lane caught his arm and steadied him.

"I otay." The little boy shrugged off Lane's hold and shot him a withering stare.

Smile returning, Julia snapped another picture. She'd make Tate's the best baby book ever.

"All right, enough." Lane rolled his eyes. "Or at least let me take some incriminating photos of you."

"You'll get your chance, I'm sure." She wiped away another escaping tear.

Lane studied her. "Are you okay?"

"Just…so many memories." Willing a semblance of composure, she motioned toward her vehicle. "I brought bedding and food bowls for Rowena. There's a big sack of dog food, too. Want to give me a hand?"

"Wait—you're leaving her here? I thought this was only a get-acquainted visit."

"You can have the rest of today, tonight and all day tomorrow to get even better acquainted. As soon as I get off work tomorrow, I'll drive up to see how it's going and check Rowena's leg."

"And then you'll take her back with you?"

She replied with a vague lift of her brow. "As I said, we'll see how it's going."

When it came to dogs, Lane's little grandson seemed to be a natural. He must take after the Frasier branch of his family tree in that regard, because the boy sure didn't get it from the Bromleys.

With Tate happily walking Rowena around the yard, Julia had taken a seat on the bottom step. Lane rested an elbow on the banister. "They make quite a pair, I have to admit."

"Don't they, though?" Julia scooted over. "Join me? I can fill you in about Rowena's routine."

Gritting his teeth against a resigned sigh, Lane sank down next to her. When his shoulder brushed hers, a tingle ran down his arm. He scrubbed it roughly with his other hand.

Julia offered a concerned frown. "Did you get into some poison ivy in the woods yesterday?"

"No." He locked his hands between his knees. "You were saying?"

She spent a few minutes outlining the dog's daily care, how much to feed her, how often to let her out for potty breaks. "And you should put her bed in your room at night so she'll feel safe."

"She's the size of a full-grown timber wolf. What's she got to be afraid of?"

The bossy veterinarian's narrow-eyed stare could have singed his eyebrows. "How would *you* feel if you'd been abandoned, hit by a car and put through major surgery to save your shattered leg?"

He grimaced. "Point taken."

Her expression softened. "Just give her lots of affection and TLC, and you'll have a friend for life."

"Gammy! Gampy!" Tugging on the leash, Tate led Rowena to the foot of the steps. One arm wrapped around the big dog's neck, he beamed a mile-wide grin. "Dis my doggy now?"

Lane glared at Julia. "This was your plan all along, wasn't it?"

She merely snickered.

He let out a long, slow breath. "Well, Tater Tot, if you promise to help me take care of this walking shag carpet, I guess we can let her stay. For now, anyway," he added with a sharp glance at Julia.

"Yay! Yay! Yay!" The kid bounced on his toes. "I wuv Weena!"

"I'm so glad, honey," Julia said as she pushed up from the step. "But Rowena's still getting better from her accident, so maybe we should take her inside and let her rest for a bit."

Tate stooped to inspect the dog's blue cast, then gave her a kiss on the ear. "Weena has owie. Poor Weena."

While Julia helped Tate guide the limping dog up to the deck, Lane grabbed the sack of food and other dog paraphernalia from Julia's SUV. No way could he say no to the dog now. He hadn't seen Tate smile that big in the whole three weeks he'd been here. And not once since Lane had picked him up at Julia's earlier had the kid asked about his mom.

Julia met him in the living room and took the dog bowls from him. "Shall I put her dishes by the pantry door?"

"Sure, why not? It'll be convenient for when I need to haul out this two-ton sack of food."

"Oh, stop bellyaching." She rolled her eyes and started for the kitchen. "Set her bed in front of the woodstove for now. The warmth will be good for her."

"Yes, your majesty." He didn't think she'd heard the murmured remark until she lasered him with another piercing stare.

No sooner had he placed the giant-size foam bed near the stove than Rowena stepped onto it, circled a couple of times and stretched out on her side with a contented sigh.

"Aw, Weena sweepy." Tate knelt beside her and gently rested his cheek against her shoulder, one hand stroking her neck.

Lane edged closer, ready to rescue his grandson at the first hint of a growl or snap. But Rowena merely lifted her head to lick Tate's nose and then lay back down. With a giggle, the boy snuggled beneath her foreleg and closed his eyes.

Coming up beside Lane, Julia smiled. "Looks like they're both ready for a nap."

"You're absolutely sure he's safe with her?"

She already had her phone out to snap a photo. "I'd certainly keep an eye on them for now, but from the looks of things, you have nothing to worry about."

Arms crossed, he swiveled to face her. "So if I let the dog stay, does it mean you'll quit bugging me about taking Tate to live with you?"

"Well, I..." Lips tight, she tucked her phone away. "I do still have some details to work out."

"That's what I thought."

"But so do you." Heaving a groan, she trudged to the sofa and slumped against the cushions. "The fact is neither of us is currently in the best position to parent a toddler. And it isn't fair to Tate."

He marched over and faced her across the coffee table. "I still think I'm better equipped than you are. For one thing, I'm not tied up with a full-time job. I'm right here pretty much 24/7."

"But can you really keep him safe while you're splitting logs or working in your woodshop or hunting elk or...or... whatever other potentially dangerous chores living off the grid requires?"

"I managed with Shannon, didn't I?"

"Not without a lot of help from your neighbors, as I recall. And that was twenty-plus years ago. I'm guessing you're around fifty now, and you're not getting any younger."

"Neither are you," he blurted, and immediately regretted it. Rugged mountain living had definitely taken a toll on his appearance, whereas city girl Julia Frasier hardly looked a day over thirty-five. Even those deepening worry lines around her eyes couldn't detract from her striking dark-haired good looks.

You need to nip this line of thinking in the bud right now, Bromley. Stay focused on the goal—keeping your grandson right where he belongs.

With a glance at the little boy, now sound asleep next to Rowena and looking as peaceful as he'd ever seen him, Lane sank onto the ottoman. "Look, Julia, I'm tired of going back and forth with you about this. For now, can't we let things be? Tate's happy here—even more so now that you've foisted this dog on us. Besides, you know I'd never let anything happen to him."

She opened her mouth as if to continue the argument but then snapped it shut and looked away. "Fine. I'll drop it for now, but only until I get things under control at the clinic. You'll never convince me Tate wouldn't be better off in town with me."

"Then maybe I'll have to do something about that."

Studying him, she asked slowly, "Like what?"

He'd surprised himself with the flippant remark, so now he needed to stall while he figured out exactly what it would take to put an end to this toddler tug-of-war.

"Well, for one thing," he began, an idea clicking into place, "I could file for custody."

"You wouldn't." Her reply came out in a menacing growl.

"Why not? Considering Shannon entrusted him with me while she's hospitalized, I doubt I'd have any trouble convincing a judge to make it official."

Julia stood abruptly. "You'd really do that? Just to keep me away from my grandson?"

"Not to keep you away, no." He hadn't meant his words to come across as a threat...or had he? His gaze drifted to the sleeping Tate. "The truth is, I should have applied for temporary guardianship as soon as Shannon was admitted."

"I can get a lawyer, too, you know. And I'd have just as much right."

Palms upraised, Lane stepped around the coffee table. "Please, I don't want to fight with you in court or out. Legal guardianship would be strictly for Tate's protection while Shannon is unable to take care of him."

"And obviously you'd have a double advantage—as Shannon's father and as a former attorney yourself."

He flinched. "How did you—"

"Yes, I looked into your background. Why shouldn't I know something about Tate's other grandparent?"

A bitter taste rose in his throat. He wanted to be angry at her for snooping, but he couldn't deny her point. "Great. What else did you learn about me?"

"I… I know about your wife." She closed her eyes briefly, her expression softening. "Lane, I'm sorry, truly. I can understand why you'd want to turn your back on that part of your life, why you brought your daughter up here where you thought she'd be safe."

He heard the *but* in her tone. "Go on, say it. If I hadn't been so overprotective with Shannon, she might not be where she is now. And you're afraid I'll do the same with Tate."

"No, I think you're smarter than that. And that's why I believe you'll think with your head instead of your heart this time."

"Because that's worked so well for you, right?" He scoffed. "This from the woman who had no idea her own son was married with a baby on the way. I have to wonder why he never got around to telling you."

Chin quivering, she snatched up her purse. "I think I should go."

"Julia, wait." He caught up with her as she fumbled with the door latch. "I was out of line. I'm the last person who should blame any parent for lack of communication with their kid."

"But you're not wrong." She pressed her forehead against the closed door. "I've asked myself a million times why Steven didn't think he could talk to me about any of this. It kills me to realize I may never get answers now."

The pain in her voice ripped through Lane's chest. A part of him wanted to take her in his arms and tell her it'd be okay, just like little Tate had an uncanny knack for doing. But reassuring words weren't going to fix things. Neither would telling himself all the choices he'd made had been for Shannon's sake. What else could either of them do now except deal with the present and hope to do better for their grandson?

"Please," he said. "Don't go yet. Not like this, anyway. Besides, don't you want to be here when Tate wakes from his nap? He'll miss you if you're gone already."

"He'll be fine, and I've obviously overstayed my welcome." Straightening, she opened the door and stepped through without looking back. "I'll check with you tomorrow to see how Rowena's doing."

Watching her drive away, he berated himself for ruining the afternoon. If only he weren't so stubborn. If only he'd learn to bend a little...

Chapter Six

"Julia, take a break." Her mother, in for the afternoon to take care of some office work, snagged Julia's elbow as she rushed from one exam room to another.

"I can't, Mom. Did you see the waiting room? That emergency bowel obstruction put us behind by a good two hours."

"And you won't be of use to anyone if you don't take care of yourself." With a glance over her shoulder, she continued in a whisper, "I know you stepped in to assist with two of your dad's appointments. Then you skipped lunch for another interview."

"Yes, so you and Dad can both eventually retire with peace of mind." She forced a smile and eased her arm free. "Excuse me, but I really need to get to my next patient."

Before Julia could reach for the chart, her mother grabbed it and perused the details. "This is a routine checkup and annual vaccines. I'll handle it. And you, my dear, will get something to eat and put your feet up for fifteen minutes."

"Mom—"

Her mother breezed through the exam room door and closed it firmly behind her, leaving Julia gaping in the corridor. She debated between following her mother's orders or heading up front to call the next patient.

Her growling stomach and a glance at her watch—*it's 3:17 already?*—made the decision for her. After a detour to the break room for a container of blueberry yogurt and a coffee refill, she ensconced herself behind her desk and kicked off her shoes. After the day she'd had, it did feel good to finally draw a full breath.

Today's lunchtime interview held promise, anyway. Currently living and working in Billings, Dr. Gene Kruger had twelve years' experience and excellent references. He needed to relocate to Missoula for family reasons, but he'd promised one month's notice before leaving his current position. Julia only hoped she could hold out that long—and in the meantime hire a reliable office manager and possibly one more vet.

As she swallowed the last spoonful of yogurt, her thoughts drifted to the big gray wolfhound…and to yesterday's disastrous end to the afternoon with Lane. Could they have been any more hurtful to each other? How was it that discussing the fate of one precious little boy could so easily bring out the worst in them?

As much as she preferred to avoid risking another argument, she did have a responsibility to the dog, and she'd told Lane she'd follow up today. Her only consolation was that weak cell service on the mountain meant she didn't have to actually speak with him.

Taking out her phone, she composed a text: Checking on Rowena. I'll come for her if necessary, but it will be much later. Busy day at the clinic.

The text showed *delivered*, and then she watched those three little dots come and go, suggesting he was composing a reply.

We're good, came the response. Leg looks okay, plenty of food. I'll text if any problems. Otherwise, check back in a few days.

A few days? Yesterday, he'd been apprehensive about keeping the dog for a single night. Guess he was equally averse to another clash of grandparent egos.

Or maybe he was already following through with his threat to gain custody of Tate. Right. Keep Grammy Frasier at arm's length until he had all the official paperwork in place. Maybe he needed another reminder that he'd sought her out so they could collaborate on how best to care for the grandson they shared.

Nothing she could do about it at the moment, and she had plenty more patients to see before closing time.

Before she could drag herself from the chair, the intercom buzzed, followed by Dylan's voice. "Call on line two, Dr. J. It's a doctor from Mercy Cottage."

Wasn't that where Lane had admitted Shannon? But why would they be calling here?

She picked up the receiver. "This is Julia Frasier."

The caller identified herself as Dr. Irene Yoshida. "Shannon Halsey is my patient, and I understand she was married to your son, Steven."

"Yes, that's correct. I've never met Shannon, though." Then she blurted, "Actually, I never even knew about the marriage until three weeks ago."

"So I was told," the doctor said softly. "Shannon has recently expressed a desire to connect with her late husband's family, and I believe it would be helpful in her recovery if you could join us for one of our sessions. Would you be willing to do that?"

"I… I suppose so." She touched a hand to her throat. "When did you have in mind?"

"Possibly Thursday morning? I'd like to prepare Shannon for the meeting. And I'm sure you may need to prepare yourself." Tenderness laced the woman's tone. "I expect this will be very emotional for both of you."

No doubt about that. Julia opened the appointment calendar

on her computer. Thursday morning looked fairly routine, and Mom probably wouldn't mind covering for her. "What time should I be there?"

"How does ten fifteen sound?"

"I'll make it work."

"That's wonderful. Thank you." Dr. Yoshida explained how to check in with reception and briefly what to expect during the session.

With her pulse thrumming, Julia couldn't guarantee she'd remember everything, but she attempted to respond appropriately. Hanging up, she wondered if Lane knew about his daughter's request. Not that he'd have any reason to object. Shannon had every right to want to meet her mother-in-law. And Julia certainly wanted to get to know the woman her son had loved and married and fathered a child with.

Fist knotted, she swiveled toward the credenza, her gaze drawn to Steven's photo. "Why?" she murmured. "Why did you think you couldn't tell me?"

After responding to the text from Julia, Lane buckled Tate into his car seat and drove partway down the mountain. For a conversation with his attorney, he needed reliable cell service.

"So what do you think, Harry? Is it doable?"

Harry Rowe, his former colleague at Clarkson, Glass and Howitt, hemmed and hawed for a moment. "Do I think you have a case? Possibly. But are you sure you want to go for full custody?"

"Shannon's doctor doesn't think she'll be getting out of the hospital any time soon, so I need to ensure my rights to make any and all decisions regarding my grandson." He glanced over his shoulder at Tate, who was paging through a story-book. He hoped the kid wasn't picking up on the gist of this conversation.

"There's a better likelihood of gaining temporary guardianship," Harry said. "It could be granted for up to six months, after which time it can be reassessed and extended if necessary." He paused. "As for your daughter, have you considered some level of conservatorship? It would strictly be for her protection."

Lane's legal career had focused on tax law and estate planning, so he wasn't up on the finer points of family law. "I hadn't thought of that. Can you get the ball rolling for me... on both counts?"

"I strongly advise you attempt to get your daughter's agreement first. Because if she resists, standing against her in court could have unpleasant ramifications."

"I hear you." Lane massaged his temple. Somehow, he'd have to make Shannon understand this was all for the best—both for her sake and for her son's.

"Gampy," Tate demanded from the rear seat. "Go home see Weena."

"In a minute, Tater Tot." He hadn't meant to sound so snappish. To Harry, he said, "Just...draw up a plan and get back to me, okay? The sooner, the better."

Over the next few days, life fell into a surprisingly comfortable rhythm. Lane hadn't thought having a dog around would turn out so well, but with Rowena helping to keep Tate entertained, it was proving easier to handle daily chores plus get some work done in his woodshop.

Should he be concerned that Julia hadn't been in touch since Monday? Either she'd stayed too busy at the clinic or she was outright avoiding him. Not that he could blame her after last Sunday. They definitely knew how to ruffle each other's feathers.

Like it or not, Bromley, you miss her.

More than he wanted to admit.

Late Wednesday afternoon, Harry texted to say he'd drawn

up preliminary paperwork for Lane to look over and asked if he could make it into town first thing Thursday. Lane enlisted Lila Vernon to watch Tate, but once she grasped the purpose of Lane's trip into Missoula, she didn't hold back her opinions. "You're playing with fire, you know. No matter how good your intentions."

"It's only temporary, just until Shannon's better. She'll un-understand." *He hoped.*

He scooped up Tate for a goodbye hug. Warm and snuggly in his footed jammies, the little boy still smelled of the lavender baby lotion Lane had applied after his bath last night.

Tate patted Lane's whiskery cheek. "I go see Mama?"

"Not today, kiddo. Maybe soon." He set him down. "Be good for Aunt Lila, and take care of Rowena, okay?"

"I be good, Gampy." One eye narrowed, Tate jabbed a pudgy finger in his direction. "Gampy be good, too."

Lila chuckled. "That'll be the day." She reached for Tate's hand. "Let's go get you some breakfast, little man."

By eight twenty, Lane was sitting at a conference table with Harry Rowe while the attorney explained the documents he'd drafted and what the process would involve. Lane wasn't so far removed from practicing law that the details were over his head, but he was glad for Harry's expertise.

Forty-five minutes later, he sat back with a sharp exhalation. "How long to set all this in motion?"

Harry toyed with a pen. "I take it you haven't discussed any of this with your daughter yet."

"As soon as we finish here, I'll head over to Mercy Cottage. I'm hoping Shannon's doctor will help me convince her."

"Good. With Shannon's cooperation, I know a judge who might be willing to move things along quickly, especially considering you're already acting as your grandson's caregiver."

"Okay, then. I'll call you once I get everything squared away."

Lane's reply held more confidence than he felt. His stomach heaved just thinking about how Shannon might react. He had to remind himself that at her lowest point, she'd chosen to come home to him. That had to count for something, despite their years-long estrangement.

Even so, as he signed the Mercy Cottage visitors' log a few minutes before ten, his hands were so slick with perspiration that he could barely grip the pen.

The receptionist consulted her computer screen and then smiled up at Lane. "Dr. Yoshida is in session with Shannon right now. It may be another hour or so, but if you don't mind waiting, I'll inform the doctor you're here."

With Lila available to watch Tate all morning, waiting made more sense than arranging a time to come back later. Besides, he needed to get this guardianship thing moving forward. He nodded and took a seat.

Too jumpy to sit for long, he was soon pacing in front of the windows. When he glimpsed a familiar lime-green SUV pull into the parking area, his heart lifted briefly before questions and doubts kicked in. What was Julia doing here? Had she been here before? Was she already conspiring with Shannon to gain custody of Tate?

As she strode toward the entrance, she slowed near his truck and then halted abruptly. After giving it a thoughtful stare, she swung her head around until her piercing brown gaze collided with Lane's through the window glass.

He waited stiffly while the receptionist buzzed Julia in. She barely glanced his way as she approached the front desk.

"You're a few minutes early, Dr. Frasier," the receptionist said. "Make yourself comfortable, and Dr. Yoshida will call you back shortly."

Giving a nod, Julia turned toward the waiting area. She cast Lane an uneasy smile. "I didn't realize you'd be here."

He tipped his head toward the front desk. "I gather you were expected?"

She looked away briefly and adjusted the shoulder strap of her purse. "Shannon asked to meet me. Her doctor called me a few days ago to set this up."

Which meant she *hadn't* been plotting against him. Now he felt ridiculously paranoid.

Julia folded her arms. "Do you have a problem with my being here?"

"No." Actually, he had all kinds of feelings about her being here, but those could be a little hard to explain. "It's just—"

The inner door opened. An attendant in a white shirt and khaki slacks, obviously the staff uniform of the day, peeked out. "Julia Frasier? Dr. Yoshida is ready for you."

Drawing a shaky breath, she squared her shoulders and marched through. When the door whispered shut behind her, Lane was left feeling snubbed and resentful. He dropped down hard onto the nearest chair. What was wrong with him, anyway, that he'd begrudge his own daughter the chance to meet her late husband's mother?

As he hauled in several steadying breaths, his gaze lifted to a plaque he hadn't noticed before. Centered over the inner doors, it read, "Mercy unto you, and peace, and love, be multiplied.—Jude 2."

That stopped him cold. Moments of genuine peace had been few and far between these past few weeks—the last twenty-plus years, if he were honest. As for his current intentions, he couldn't be sure whether they were loving or merely selfish.

And mercy? For too long, it had been just a word to him. Abstract, intangible, mysterious.

Not for the first time, he pondered the fact that if he'd gone to the office for that forgotten file instead of sending Tessa, she'd still be alive. Even if he'd been shot and killed instead, their daughter wouldn't have grown up without a mother.

Can you ever forgive me, Tessa? Can our daughter?

He recalled his initial conversation with Dr. Yoshida the day he'd admitted Shannon. The first thing the slender, raven-haired doctor had suggested was that they pray together. Still too numb with shock to explain he put no stock in prayer, he'd nodded distractedly, ready to get the whole process over with. Now the closing words of Dr. Yoshida's prayer filled his thoughts: *Holy Lord, Your love is everlasting, and Your peace is beyond comprehension. In mercy may You surround, heal and uphold this family, today and always.*

Whether it was merely the words themselves or something—*Someone?*—more, he sensed the tiniest measure of that longed-for peace.

He didn't deserve it, didn't understand it, but maybe he didn't have to. Maybe that was the truest meaning of mercy.

Julia had both longed for and dreaded this meeting. The one thought tormenting her more than all others was that Shannon knew more about the last years of Steven's life—his hopes, his plans, his loves, his losses—than Julia might ever learn.

A dark-haired woman wearing tortoiseshell glasses greeted her in the corridor. "Hello, I'm Irene Yoshida. Thank you for coming." She offered her hand. "May I call you Julia?"

"Please." Accepting the polite handshake, she glanced past the doctor into an empty sunlit office.

"I'll have Shannon join us shortly," the doctor said as if reading the question in Julia's eyes. "First, I'd like to chat with you for a few minutes."

Dr. Yoshida showed Julia to a cozy sitting area at one end of the spacious room. When the doctor offered coffee, Julia accepted out of habit and then wished she hadn't. A jolt of caffeine wouldn't do her jangling nerves any favors. Sipping sparingly, she tried to smile as she replied to casual but clearly intentional questions about her work at the clinic, how long she'd lived in the Missoula area, how she'd managed as a single mom. Shannon must have mentioned the fact that Steven's parents were divorced.

"It wasn't easy," Julia replied, "but I had a lot of help from my mom and dad."

"I'm sure." The doctor's smile warmed. "Tell me more about your son."

"He— He was—" Her throat closed. She snatched a tissue from the box on an end table and pressed it beneath her eyes. "Sorry."

Leaning closer, Dr. Yoshida touched Julia's knee. "Never apologize for grief."

"I thought after two years it wouldn't hurt so much. But now…"

"Now you have a daughter-in-law you've never met and a grandson you never expected."

"Exactly." Voice breaking, she murmured, "It makes me wonder if I ever knew my son at all."

"Of course you knew him. But every child must eventually find his or her own way in the world. And if we look closely," the doctor continued with a thoughtful tilt of her head, "we will see our own reflections mirrored in the lives they have forged."

Julia was beginning to feel like *she* was the one in therapy. "So I'm the reason my son kept his marriage from me? It's my fault he couldn't tell me he was about to become a father?"

"Those are troubling questions, to be sure, and I'm sorry I can't offer answers." The doctor stood and moved toward the door. "I think it's time for you to meet Shannon. I sense

God has a plan for you to find strength in each other on this path toward healing."

God? A plan? Right. Then where had He been all these years?

Julia barely had time to process the absurd thought before Dr. Yoshida reappeared, her arm around the shoulders of a pale, slender blonde. "Shannon, this is Steven's mother."

Julia stood, her heart suddenly so full she could hardly breathe. This was her son's wife, the mother of her grandson. *My daughter-in-law.*

"Hi," she said, her voice a mere tremor. "I'm Julia."

As if in slow motion, the girl stumbled toward her and threw her arms around her neck. "I miss him. I miss him so much!"

She returned Shannon's embrace, their tears mingling. "I know, I know. I do, too."

"He'd be so mad at me right now."

Julia tipped her head back to peer into Shannon's eyes. "Oh, honey, why would you think such a thing?"

"Because I can't take care of our son. I can't even take care of myself."

She pressed Shannon close. "Steven would understand how hard it's been, everything you've had to face without him. He—" she choked back a sob "—he was the most forgiving, caring person I ever knew."

Shannon's head jerked up and down in fierce agreement. "That's why I need him, why I can't go on without him."

"Honey, you have to." She gave the girl's shoulder a reassuring rub. "That's why your dad brought you here, so you can get well and get back to being Tate's mom."

The girl shifted, tilting her tear-streaked face to look up at Julia. A smile lifted the corners of her mouth. "I get it now. You're the answer to my prayer."

"What?" She glanced across the room to where Dr. Yoshida

observed from a distance. The woman's brows lifted, whether in concern or curiosity, Julia couldn't tell.

Gripping Julia's hands, Shannon tugged her over to a settee. "I only came home to my dad's because I was sick and desperate and didn't know where else to go. But now I'm in here, and Tate's up there on the mountain with him—"

"If you're worried about Tate, I promise you, he's doing fine."

"You don't understand." Shannon's voice rose. "I don't know how long I'm going to be here, and I can't bear the thought of my little boy so...so *alone* up there." Her fingers tightened around Julia's. "But you could take him. You could keep him until I'm well. Please—"

Dr. Yoshida strode over. "Shannon, remember how you've been practicing to stay calm."

Trembling, the girl nodded. Hand to her chest, she inhaled through her nose, then blew out slowly through pursed lips. "Sorry. I just— I just—"

"It's okay," Julia soothed. She didn't dare say aloud how much she'd been hoping for the very thing Shannon was asking of her. "I know it's hard being away from your son, but it's obvious your dad loves him very, very much. I visit them every chance I get." Remembering the photos she'd taken of Tate last Sunday, she tugged her phone from her purse. "Look, Tate has a new friend. This is Rowena."

Shannon's eyes brightened even as fresh tears fell. "My baby boy has a dog." A tiny laugh bubbled up as she touched the image of Tate hugging Rowena's neck. "She's so big."

"But gentle as can be." Julia's throat tightened. "Steven always loved big dogs, too."

It was the wrong thing to say. Doubling over, Shannon hugged her knees and burst into uncontrollable sobs. Dr. Yoshida stepped into the corridor briefly, and moments later, two attendants gently escorted Shannon from the room.

Julia stood on shaky legs. "I'm so sorry."

"Not your fault. Such breakdowns are all part of the healing process." The doctor glanced at her watch. "I've been informed Shannon's father has come to visit her but wants to discuss something with me first. It would be of value to Shannon's plan of care if I could speak with you and Mr. Bromley together. Would you mind?"

"I suppose not." What else could she say?

A few moments later, Lane lowered himself into the chair next to hers. Jaw muscles bunching beneath his whiskers, he shot Julia a quick glance before addressing Dr. Yoshida. "I'd prefer to talk with you privately concerning a, uh, personal matter I need to handle with Shannon."

The back of Julia's neck tingled. "If this involves Tate, I think I'd better hear it, too."

Before the doctor could comment, an attendant called her to the door. Turning to Lane and Julia, she apologized that she had a "patient situation" to deal with and would have to postpone their conversation until a better time.

Julia only hoped the patient involved wasn't Shannon. She'd never witnessed such brokenness in another human being. After Steven's death, she'd denied herself the consolation of a full-blown meltdown—not in front of her parents, and most certainly not with the church-sponsored grief support group they'd dragged her to. One meeting, and she was out of there.

Lane's touch to her arm pulled her out of the memories. "Julia? You okay?"

"Yes, I'm fine." Squaring her shoulders, she faced him. "I fervently hope this 'personal matter' you referred to isn't what you brought up last Sunday. Because it would be a huge mistake."

Chapter Seven

❧

Lane's fragmentary peace was long gone. He met Julia's glare with one of his own. "How is it a mistake to want to protect my daughter and her son?"

"Of course you want to protect them. So do I." Looking toward the door, she shuddered. "But if you could just for a moment grasp a mother's fierce love, the all-consuming drive to ensure your child's future, to protect him from everything you couldn't control about your own life…"

He suspected she wasn't merely talking about Shannon. Even so, he got the message loud and clear, and it hurt. "She told you she doesn't want me keeping Tate."

Her eyes fell shut. "Yes."

He strode to the window. It was a bright morning, sunlight glinting off the windshields in the parking lot, a breeze stirring leaves just beginning to turn. How could the world appear so calm out there when here in this room he felt like his insides were being ripped apart?

How much more damage can you do to the daughter you profess to love?

He reached into the inside pocket of his jacket and removed the thick brown envelope containing the documents Harry had prepared. Without a word, he handed it to Julia.

She cast him a dubious frown. "What's this?"

"Exactly what you think. Almost, anyway." Sinking into

his chair, he palmed his eye sockets. "I'm only trying to look out for my daughter and grandson. *Our* grandson."

Papers rustling told him Julia had opened the envelope. He kept his head down as she perused the contents.

Just when he couldn't bear the silence any longer, she murmured, "I hate to say it, but this makes sense."

He swung around to face her. "You mean it?"

"Yes, I do." Acquiescence softened her tone. "Someone does need to manage Shannon's affairs while she's hospitalized. And someone needs the legal authority to make care decisions for Tate."

"But apparently, Shannon doesn't want that *someone* to be me." Lane sank deeper into the chair. "And if I push her on this, she'll hate me more than she already does."

"She doesn't hate you, Lane."

"How do you know?"

"Because when she hit rock bottom, you're the one she came to." Julia touched his arm. "You're her dad. You'll always be her dad."

"The dad who failed her. We've already established I'm to blame for driving her away in the first place."

"Stop right there." She gave his arm a shake. "Dwelling on whatever mistakes you made in the past isn't helping Shannon or you, and especially not Tate. All that matters is doing the right thing now."

"Which is…what? Because where my daughter's concerned, I'm not exactly batting a thousand."

The legal documents rested on her lap. She tapped the stack with her index finger. "This, right here. But with one small change, if you're willing."

He studied her. "I'm listening."

"Include me as co-guardian."

The suggestion threw him for a moment. "How would

that work, exactly? I mean—" sarcasm entered his tone "—considering how you and I are always so much in agreement."

Wincing, she glanced away. "I know I can be opinionated and somewhat controlling—"

"You mean bossy?" He couldn't stifle a chuckle. When she glared at him, he swiveled to gently seize her wrists. "Hey, I need 'bossy' sometimes to counteract my own stubbornness."

That brought a smile from her. "At least you finally admitted it."

"So we've both got our faults." Suddenly conscious of their physical closeness, he released his hold on her and sat back. "If joint guardianship is even a legal option, we'll have to do a better job of communicating."

"I promise to try if you will."

The door eased open, and Dr. Yoshida stepped in. "Oh, you're both still here."

"Sorry, we got to talking," Julia said as she and Lane stood. "We'll get out of your way."

"If you can stay a little longer, I have time now for our conversation." When all were seated again, she went on, "I just came from Shannon's room. She's much calmer now, but she's had an emotionally exhausting morning. I'm sorry, Mr. Bromley, but it might be better to visit her another time."

"Of course. Whatever's best for my daughter."

Dr. Yoshida adjusted her glasses. "I believe you had something specific in mind when you asked to see me."

"I did, but…" He glanced over at Julia.

"Before you returned," she supplied, "we were discussing temporary guardianship for Tate. Also, Lane has consulted an attorney about establishing a conservatorship for Shannon while she's in treatment." She passed the document across to the doctor.

After taking a few moments to look it over, Dr. Yoshida

nodded. "Many of our patients have such arrangements with family members. I can certainly talk about this with Shannon and help her understand the implications."

"It's only until she gets well," Lane stated. "Please assure her I'm not trying to take over her life. And same with Tate's guardianship." He explained he and Julia would be looking into a shared arrangement.

"I'm sure that would be a relief for Shannon. I hope you can work out the details." The doctor stood. "I'll be in touch about this soon. I'd also like to arrange for you to bring Tate one day next week. By then, I believe Shannon will be emotionally ready for some time with her little boy."

"That'd be great," Lane said as the doctor held the door for them. "Tate's really been missing his mom."

At the threshold, Julia paused. "What about Tate's feelings? What will it do to him to have a short visit with his mother and then have to be separated from her again?"

Lane gnawed his lip. "Julia's right. It took nearly three weeks before he stopped asking for his mom several times a day—and then only after the dog came to live with us."

"Dog?" Curiosity lit Dr. Yoshida's expression.

"A stray I treated at my clinic." Julia briefly explained about Rowena and how the dog had become a companion for Tate.

"I had serious doubts at first," Lane added, "but those two are inseparable now." He shared a warm look with Julia and then had trouble tearing his gaze away.

The doctor nodded thoughtfully. "Then bring the dog with you for the visit. She'll serve both as a conversation focus and comfort for Tate when it's time to return home."

"Okay, we'll give it a try."

Julia was happily surprised at the way her trip to Mercy Cottage had concluded. Could she and Lane have finally reached the point of declaring a truce? His heart was in the right place. She'd never doubted that. And she was slowly becoming resigned to the fact that Tate should stay at Lane's for the time being. However, if this shared guardianship thing worked out, at least she'd have a say in whatever decisions needed to be made.

On their way out to the parking area, Lane said he'd contact his attorney friend to discuss revising the petition. "Or… maybe you'd like to go along? I can call him right now and see if he's available. We could even get some lunch somewhere on the way."

His hopeful tone, not to mention the boyish glint in those smoky green eyes, stirred something deep in Julia's chest.

Admit it, he's burrowing a little deeper under your skin every time you're around him.

But she needed to be sensible. There was no room in her life to entertain anything resembling romantic interest, whether with Lane Bromley or anyone else on her radar.

Except there was no one else. She hadn't allowed anyone this close since Steven's dad had thoroughly let her down—let them *both* down.

Lane scuffed his boot heel on the sidewalk. "Forget it. I know you're busy."

Wincing, she glanced away. "My mom's been covering for me at the clinic, and I really need to get back."

"And I should head home to relieve Lila. I hadn't expected to be gone this long."

"Well, there you have it. Two busy people with things to do and places to be." Her lighthearted lilt was the only defense against the part of her that wanted to throw obligation to the wind and find out what, if anything, could come of this reluctant friendship.

"Okay, well…have a good day." He cringed the instant the words left his mouth. "Wow. How corny did *that* sound?"

Corny actually looked pretty cute on the guy. Hiding her smile, Julia moved toward her SUV. "You have a good day, too. Give Tate a hug from Grammy, and tell him I'll come see him in a couple of days."

"I'll do that. And…Julia?"

She met his gaze over her open car door. "Yes?"

"The guest room's yours anytime you want to stay for the weekend."

"And risk getting snowed in again?" She shivered just thinking about it—and *not* because of feeling cold. Nope, it was forced proximity with an all-too-attractive mountain man. "Not sure I want to chance it."

He shrugged. "Just offering."

Hard to believe the man used to be a lawyer. Weren't they supposed to have poker faces? Lane Bromley wore his emotions too close to the surface, and right now, disappointment was written all over his face.

Great. The obvious signs were getting harder to ignore. She could tell he was starting to like her, too. Could this relationship get any more complicated?

Sliding behind the wheel, she called, "Keep me posted about the guardianship plan. I'll be in touch about visiting Tate this weekend."

She glimpsed his half-hearted wave as she backed out of her parking spot, and then his wide-mouthed stare an instant before a car horn blared. She slammed on the brakes in time to miss crashing into a minivan. Hands shaking, she watched in the rearview mirror for the van to go on by.

A tap on her side window startled her. It was Lane. "You okay?"

She lowered the window. "Other than slightly embarrassed? A few too many things on my mind, apparently."

"Just be careful." A half smile turned up one corner of his mouth. "Tate needs both his grandparents around."

Returning his smile, she began to relax. They could do this. Whatever differences lay between them, wherever this inconvenient—and apparently mutual—attraction might lead, they could handle anything for the sake of their precious grandson.

Julia's phone vibrated as she moved between patient rooms on Friday afternoon. She snatched it from her lab coat pocket and read the incoming text from Lane: Update from my attorney. We need to talk. Coming up tomorrow?

Could he be any more cryptic? Since yesterday, she'd done her best to put both Lane and the co-guardianship idea out of her mind. It was exhausting enough managing her patient load while also reviewing résumés and discreetly keeping an eye on her dad. Now Lane had her worried that their idea had hit a snag.

Dylan passed her in the hallway and then backtracked. He glanced in both directions before facing her. "I was in an exam room with your dad a few minutes ago, and…he's not looking so good."

She stiffened. "What do you mean?"

"Several of us have noticed his hands shaking," Dylan whispered. "Amy said you've been keeping it on the down-low, and we want to respect his privacy. But for a moment just now, his speech seemed a little slurred. He laughed it off and recovered quickly, but you should get him to see a doctor."

"Yes, I know." Her stomach twisted. How much longer could she count on the staff's discretion?

How much longer before something went disastrously wrong and they were caught up in a costly malpractice suit? Even worse, what if these minor episodes her father seemed determined to ignore proved to be signs of a far more serious health condition?

She touched Dylan's arm. "Thank you for coming to me. Please assure the staff that my mother and I are keeping a close eye on the situation. If anyone ever feels at all uneasy about my father's ability to treat a patient, don't hesitate to ask me or my mother to step in."

"I understand. If there's anything any of us can do to help, just ask." He started to go, then turned back to say, "It'll all work out, Dr. J. We're praying for your dad. And for you."

"Th-thanks," she murmured, realizing only after Dylan had walked away that she meant it.

Usually, when anyone mentioned they'd be praying for her, a sour taste rose in her mouth. Those were just empty words and false comfort. But since yesterday, she hadn't been able to stop thinking about Dr. Yoshida's remark that God had a plan for her and Shannon. And then Shannon's unexpected words, *You're the answer to my prayer…*

How could she be *anyone's* answered prayer when she could barely manage her own hectic life?

The exam room door in front of her cracked open, and Amy peeked out. "Lucy's ready for you, Dr. J. It looks like an eye infection."

"Be right in. I, uh, just need to…um…" She looked down at the hand clutching her cell phone. It was shaking harder than she'd ever observed her father's tremble. She thrust both hands into her pockets. "Excuse me," she muttered, and fled to her office. Slamming the door, she collapsed against it.

What is wrong with me? She never used to get this rattled. She was always the one people came to when they needed clear thinking and an orderly plan of action.

Someone tapped on the door. "Dr. J, it's Amy. Sorry, but

Lucy's howling up a storm, and Mrs. Springer is getting impatient."

She swiped at her damp cheeks. "I need a minute, please."

A pause. "Can I get you anything?"

"No, thanks," she said with forced brightness. "I'll be right there."

Straightening her shoulders, she checked her appearance in the mirror behind the door. She hadn't shed enough tears to ruin her makeup, but the face staring back at her looked anything but calm and in control.

A pained laugh escaped. "Nothing a week or two at a secluded beach resort wouldn't cure."

Who are you kidding?

It would take a lot more than a tropical vacation to fix everything wrong in her life. There was no escaping her father's failing abilities or the pressure to keep the clinic up and running. She certainly couldn't duck out on her grandson. And she could never in a million years outrun her grief over losing her son.

Yet she kept trying, didn't she? She kept attempting to control everything, even her emotions. Wasn't that just another form of escapism?

On the other hand…what if all this tumult was the cosmos— *God?*—telling her it was time to try a different approach? Did she have the courage to drop the reins, to admit she didn't always have the answers, to lean on someone else instead of thinking she had to do it all?

She turned away from the woman in the mirror and reached for the doorknob. She only needed to hold it together for two more hours. Then later, alone with her thoughts and those two needy but lovable dachshunds she shared her home with, she'd figure all this out.

Or not.

* * *

In his workshop Saturday morning, Lane looked up from the bookcase he was staining and grinned at the sight of Tate playing ball with Rowena. The kid had scooted into one corner of the portable play yard and was rolling the ball across to the dog in the opposite corner. She'd gotten the hang of corralling it between her front paws and then nudging it back to him with her nose. Each time, he'd clap his hands and release one of his high-pitched giggles.

Too bad Julia had to miss this. The thought reminded him she'd never responded to his text yesterday afternoon. She wasn't going to like Harry's answer regarding co-guardianship, so Lane had decided it'd be better to explain in person. He'd assumed she'd drive up today after the clinic closed at noon, but now he was beginning to wonder. She did have a life beyond her career and her grandson…although he couldn't claim to have seen any evidence of that.

Nope, Julia Frasier was as doggedly single-minded as he was.

He snorted at his own pun. Since Rowena had joined the family, he'd discovered he was more of a dog person than he would have believed.

After finishing with the bookcase, he washed up at the work sink, collected Tate and Rowena, and headed to the cabin. While the two of them trotted ahead, he checked his phone to make sure he hadn't missed a reply from Julia.

Still nothing. He paused at the foot of the deck stairs and debated whether to text her again.

Then a motion caught his eye. He jerked his head up to see Tate already halfway up the steps and tumbling backward. The phone fell to the ground as Lane dived to catch his grandson—except Rowena beat him to it, blocking Tate's fall with her big furry body. Whether going upstairs or down, how did the dog always seem to know that she should position herself a couple of steps below Tate?

Heart thudding, and even more grateful for Rowena's presence, he leaned past her to snatch up Tate. After giving the kid a quick once-over, he clutched him against his chest. "How many times have I told you to wait for Gramps before going up the steps?"

"I sorry, Gampy." Tate freed one of his hands to pat Lane's cheek. "No be mad, otay?"

"I'm not mad, Tater Tot." He should be angry with himself for not paying closer attention. "You scared me, is all. You could have been hurt really bad."

"I not hurt. Weena save me."

"She did indeed." He made a conscious effort to slow his racing pulse and made a mental note to give the dog a big hunk of the elk steak he'd set out to thaw for tonight's supper.

Which reminded him he'd been about to try Julia again before Tate's stumble. He glanced around for his phone and found it near his boot, the screen a spiderweb of cracks. Groaning, he stooped to retrieve it.

Tate poked out his lower lip. "Uh-oh. Gampy phone have owie."

"Yep, looks like it's a goner." So much for checking in with Julia. Or anyone else, for that matter. "How about some lunch? You hungry?"

They sat down to Tate's favorite, tortillas and sliced turkey with hummus. The mixture of flavors was starting to grow on Lane, although he liked his with a dash of Tabasco. After lunch, he propped Tate on his lap in the rocking chair and read him a story before taking him upstairs for a nap. As usual, Rowena curled up on the fuzzy dog blanket he'd spread near Tate's crib. Her loyalty to the boy continued to amaze him.

Next, he puttered around the cabin, sweeping the floor,

wiping kitchen counters and dabbing water spots off the bathroom faucets. Then, just in case Julia decided to stay over—if she even made the drive up this afternoon—he freshened the spare room.

With no sign of her by midafternoon, he grew more than a little concerned. The Julia Frasier he'd come to know was prompt and organized, not to mention tenacious about ensuring Tate's well-being.

He poked at his cell phone again, confirming the thing was hopelessly dead. His communications backup was shortwave radio, not that he expected to reach Julia that way, but he could ask the Vernons to relay a text message.

Upstairs, he peeked in on Tate and Rowena, both still fast asleep, then continued down the hall to his study. As he pulled up a chair in front of the radio, his ears picked up the metallic squeal of his front gate. He darted back downstairs and out to the deck, his heart lifting at the sight of Julia's lime-green SUV turning in.

He waited at the bottom of the steps while she parked and then strode over. "I wasn't sure—"

She threw open her door and practically jumped from the vehicle. "I've been texting you since noon. Is everything okay?"

"Yeah, yeah, it's fine." Steadying her with a gentle grip on her forearms, he offered an embarrassed frown. "I had a little accident with my cell phone." Better all around if he spared her the details.

Face contorting in a mixture of relief and annoyance, she jerked her arms free. "Don't scare me like that ever again!"

"What was I supposed to do? Drive all the way into town and tell you in person just so you wouldn't worry?" Bad enough how he'd worried about *her*.

"Well, you could have— I don't know—" She turned away, her shoulders rising and falling in a long, purposeful breath.

When she faced him again, a semblance of calm had returned. A forced calm, if he was any judge, as was her tight smile. "Sorry for overreacting. Accidents happen."

He set his hands on his hips. "What's going on with you, Julia?"

"Nothing." After another deep breath and an exaggerated eye roll, she muttered, "What you've just witnessed is my attempt—and obvious failure—to stop being such a control freak."

A laugh exploded from deep in his chest. At her hurt expression, he immediately silenced it. "Tate should be waking up from his nap soon. How about we go inside and put on a pot of coffee?" Arching a brow, he added, "I'm thinking decaf."

This time, a genuine smile lifted the corners of her mouth. "That's probably wise."

Following her up the steps, he couldn't deny there was something different about her today. For one thing, she'd passed up a perfect opportunity to rake him over the coals about his broken phone and the dangers of being so isolated up here on the mountain.

But how long would her attitude adjustment last once he told her that Harry Rowe had nixed the co-guardianship idea?

Chapter Eight

"No possibility of co-guardianship? That's just great." Julia shoved up from the kitchen table and paced to the counter. Good thing they were drinking decaf, or she'd be slamming cupboard doors right now.

"Don't shoot the messenger." Lane lifted both hands. "I'm only relaying what my lawyer told me."

"And I suppose the thing about possession being nine-tenths of the law means I have zero rights where my grandson is concerned."

"Once again, Tate is and always will be *our* grandson. Anyway, that old saying has no real legal basis."

She huffed. "It's still pretty much true in this case, isn't it?"

"Julia, would you—"

"Gampy!" Tate's shrill voice echoed from upstairs. "I wake!"

Directing an exasperated frown her way, Lane excused himself.

The interruption gave Julia time to bridle her runaway temper. So far, her resolve to be less controlling wasn't going very well. Why did it always come down to a choice between commanding the situation or getting her needs and wants trampled by everyone else? There had to be middle ground, didn't there?

Hearing a trio of footsteps, she pasted on a cheerful smile for her grandson. Rowena appeared first. She stopped at the bottom of the staircase, tail wagging, and licked Tate's cheek as he hopped off the last step. Warmth flooded Julia's chest at the picture those two made. Later, she'd give the dog a quick once-over and check the cast leg.

She knelt as Tate toddled into the kitchen. "There's my sweetie pie!"

"Gammy!" He tumbled into her outstretched arms. "Miss you, Gammy."

"I missed you, too." She kissed his forehead, gripped his tiny shoulders, and looked him up and down. "Wow, I think you've grown an inch since I saw you last Sunday."

Lane made a show of massaging his lower back. "I'm pretty sure he's gained a couple of pounds."

"I big now." Tate puffed out his chest and gave it a boastful pat, eliciting laughter from both his grandparents.

While Lane made a snack for Tate, Julia returned to her chair and pulled the little boy onto her lap. "Have you had a fun week with Rowena?"

He nodded fiercely. "We p'ay ball. An' Weena save me."

"She did?" Julia knit her brow.

"Here you go, Tater Tot." Lane set a saucer of banana slices on the table, then scooped him off Julia's lap and plopped him into a chair. "And don't feed Rowena your banana. I'll get her a treat from the pantry."

"Otay, Gampy."

When Lane returned with a handful of dog treats, Julia whispered, "Rowena saved him? What's he talking about?"

"Nothing. She always keeps a close eye on him." Lane offered the treats to Rowena before sitting down and taking a swig of coffee.

Mumbling over a mouthful of banana, Tate said, "I fall an' Gampy phone got owie."

Julia gaped at Lane. "He *fell*?"

"I told you, it was nothing. You can see he's perfectly fine."

"There's clearly more to it than you're saying. How exactly did Rowena *save* him?"

Lane grimaced. Avoiding her icy stare, he described how he was distracted checking his phone, and how Tate stumbled on the steps with Rowena right behind him. "It only happened because I was worried about *you*," he said, a defiant twist to his mouth. "You never answered my text yesterday."

Julia cycled through indignation, amazement, gratitude and finally chagrin. "Yesterday wasn't one of my better days." Slanting him a look, she added, "And that's in large part thanks to you."

"Me?"

"On top of everything I was dealing with at the clinic, your cryptic message threw me for a loop. Which reminds me." She cast a wary glance at Tate, who was methodically nibbling around the edges of a banana slice. "We haven't finished our discussion."

Lane pulled a hand down his face. "I wanted the co-guardianship thing to work as much as you did. As I was about to explain before Tate woke up, for a judge to even consider it, we'd have to be married or, at the very least, living together as a couple."

"Well, *that's* never happening." She slapped the table.

Startled, Tate gaped at her. "Gammy mad?"

"No, honey." She immediately regretted the outburst. "Grammy's just feeling a little cranky."

Lane went to the sink and came back with a wet cloth to wipe Tate's mouth and fingers. "I've got even more reason to be cranky," he muttered. "I thought we'd found a solution that would placate Shannon. She'll never grant me sole guardianship, even temporarily."

Julia stifled the momentary burst of satisfaction. Her chances of having Tate live with her may have just shot up, but gloating would serve no purpose. Besides, she had yet to work herself into a position to keep him full-time, especially after what Dylan had mentioned yesterday about her father.

The reminder made her stomach knot. She and Mom couldn't keep putting off the hard conversation they needed to have with Dad. Being forced to confront his failing ability to serve their patients would break his heart, but the clinic's reputation was at stake, and Dad, more than all of them, would want its success to continue.

"So I was hoping you'd help me convince her." Lane brought over the coffee pot and topped off her mug.

She glanced up. "Sorry, what were you saying?"

"Shannon. The guardianship thing. Since she apparently trusts you more than she does me, maybe you could smooth things over about me keeping Tate until she's better."

Tate climbed down from his chair and tugged on Lane's jeans. "Go see Mama?"

"In a few more days, kiddo." Lane tousled the boy's mop of dark hair. "Hey, why don't you take Rowena to the living room? You can sit on the rug and roll the ball."

"Otay!" Tate patted the dog's side. "C'mon, Weena."

Cradling her mug, Julia rose and leaned in the archway. A wistful smile formed as she watched the boy and dog begin their game. "They are so sweet together."

"They are indeed."

Her thoughts returned to Lane's request, and she shifted to face him. "I only just met Shannon. I don't know what I could say to help your cause."

Jaw clenched, he crossed his arms. "Why? Because you'll be pushing her to grant *you* temporary guardianship?"

A week ago, even a day ago, the answer would have been a resounding yes. But now... "It pains me to admit it," she said over the growing lump in her throat, "but you've been right all along. I am presently in no position to—to take on—" Her voice broke, and she pressed a fist to her mouth.

"Hey, now." Lane stood and relieved her of the coffee mug, setting it on the table. He slid his arm around her shoulders.

She couldn't stop herself from leaning into him, and the warmth of his solid chest comforted her in a way she hadn't experienced in too long to recall.

Then awkwardness set in. Unable to look at him, she cleared her throat and stood erect. "I may have mentioned I've been a bit stressed lately."

He backed off only a small step, but to her, ridiculously, the distance felt like a chasm. He stuffed his hands into his jeans pockets. "How do we continually go off the rails with each other?"

"Good question." She dared a smile. The real question, one she couldn't ask aloud, was, what exactly was she beginning to feel for this man?

Propping himself across from her in the archway, he released a noisy breath. "We keep saying we're on the same side and both want what's best for our grandson, so let's start right there."

She cast him a pensive frown. "I'm listening."

"As I see it, even if co-guardianship isn't a legal option, it doesn't mean we can't make this work. I know you've had doubts about my ability to keep Tate safe up here on the mountain—"

"Which were only reinforced after you told me he nearly fell down the steps today."

Lane dipped his chin. "I *will* be more careful, you have my word. But since you're not able to take him right now anyway, it looks like you're going to have to trust me."

Tate's high-pitched giggle drew her attention back to the living room. He was vigorously rubbing Rowena's belly while she squirmed with pure delight and pawed the air.

Chuckling, Lane said, "That's one of their favorite games."

She sniffed to hold back a sudden spate of tears. "Moments like these…that's what makes it all so hard."

"What? Why?"

"Because of everything I'm missing out on." Now the tears fell in earnest. "Even if I were to take him, I'd have to leave him with a sitter five or six days a week. I still wouldn't be there for all the special moments." Her heart lurched. "Just like I was never there for Steven."

Closing the space between them, Lane pressed her face between his strong but gentle hands. "I don't believe that." His gaze grew tender as he thumbed away the wetness beneath her eyes. "Not for a single minute."

"But it's true. After the divorce, I started working longer and longer hours. I was a desperate single mom just trying to make ends meet and—"

"You don't have to justify yourself to me." He drew her into his arms. "Your son knew you loved him, and based on everything I've gleaned from you and Shannon, you raised him to be a kind and caring young man."

"I miss him so much!" She nestled deeper into the softness of Lane's fleece vest. He smelled of soap and woodsmoke, masculine scents that made her feel protected, secure. Before today, she'd vehemently resisted such signs of weakness—the competent, controlled, independent Julia Frasier had no need of a man to comfort her.

Yet right now, right here in Lane Bromley's arms…it was the only place she wanted to be.

How many times lately had he let his thoughts wander to visions of holding Julia exactly like this?

Well, not *quite* like this. Not with her so vulnerable, immersed in grief and regret. No, he'd pictured something a little more along the lines of two people who acknowledged their attraction to each other and were willing to chance a relationship in spite of their differences.

He grazed his lips across her forehead and felt her shiver. "Maybe we should..."

"I, um... Sorry." Sniffling, she edged away and brushed at her cheeks.

Lightly touching her elbow, he said, "We'll figure this out, Julia. Together. I don't know how exactly, but we will, because Tate needs you, and I... I need you, too."

She glanced back, brows pinched into sideways question marks.

"Well, I do." He tried to laugh off the remark, because otherwise she might read between the lines and make things *really* awkward. "I need you to hold me accountable—for both Tate and that silly dog you saddled me with."

"Oh, don't worry. I will." A glimmer of the snarky Julia he'd unexpectedly grown to care for shone through. "Which reminds me, I want to take a look at Rowena's leg before I go."

"You're not leaving any time soon, I hope. I'm grilling elk steaks for supper again."

"No arm twisting required." Smile returning, she shifted her gaze toward Tate and Rowena. "Besides, we've been so busy talking—"

He squeezed one eye shut. "Don't you mean arguing?"

"Okay, *arguing*—which I hope we can dispense with once and for all. What I was going to say is, I haven't spent enough time with that little guy today."

"Then have at it. I've got barn chores and a few other things to tend to before I start grilling. You guys can play as long as you want."

As he brushed past her, she caught his sleeve. "Lane?"

"Yeah?"

"Thank you."

Her unguarded smile made him long to kiss her—*really* kiss her this time. He swallowed hard before asking, "For what?"

"For being a friend when I needed one."

He could only nod. Then he berated himself all the way out to the barn for letting himself even think of wanting more from her. When he'd explained that co-guardianship would require them to be a committed couple, her emphatic veto had stung. He wanted to believe the swift reply had been pure reflex. He wanted to believe she'd also felt something as he'd held her.

He wanted to believe there was a reason Julia Frasier had come into his life when she did. For Tate's sake, certainly, but also because for too many years he'd desperately needed someone like Julia. Someone spirited and determined enough to drag him off this mountain—figuratively, if not literally— and back into the real world again.

Filling the cow's feed pan, he snorted. His cracked cell phone was one more reason he'd be making the trek into Missoula. Until a few weeks ago, he'd considered the phone a necessary nuisance. But finding himself suddenly cut off today had been unnerving. If Julia hadn't shown up when she did… He'd been minutes away from loading Tate and the dog into the truck and hightailing it into town to find her.

With evening chores attended to, he started back to the cabin. No doubt about it, things went much faster when he didn't have to set up Tate in the portable play yard and then try to keep one eye on him while he worked. He'd had a similar arrangement when Shannon was a toddler and managed fine—but that was twenty-plus years ago. Not that fifty qualified him as *old*, but a glance in the mirror confirmed the years were creeping up.

Years he could never get back. Mistakes he could never undo. Dreams that would forever go unfulfilled.

Tessa.

With a jolt, he realized she'd crept into his thoughts less often lately. Was it merely because he'd been preoccupied with the needs of their daughter and grandson...or because he'd begun to contemplate the future rather than regretting the unchangeable past while stagnating in the all-too-predictable present?

At the foot of the outer stairs, he glanced up to the window and saw Julia framed by the yellow-orange glow of lamplight. When she smiled and wiggled her fingers in a wave, his heart gave a tiny leap. The fatigue that had slowed his trek from the barn evaporated, and he jogged upstairs with the energy of his youth. They might be a long way from anything more than friendship, but he'd let it be enough—for now, anyway.

She met him at the door. "Thought you'd never finish out there. I'm getting hungry for that steak you promised."

"I'll fire up the grill right now."

Soon, they sat down to dinner, and by the time they finished, Tate was beginning to nod. Julia offered to get him ready for bed while Lane did the dishes. He'd just started the coffeemaker when she returned to the kitchen.

"Tate and his faithful companion are all tucked in." She rubbed her hands together. "Mmm, I smell fresh coffee."

Setting out two mugs, he grinned over his shoulder. "I can also break out my secret stash of dark chocolate, if you're interested."

Her brows shot up. "You have chocolate and this is the first I'm hearing of it? You are *so* in trouble, Lane Bromley."

As he went to the pantry, all kinds of hopeful feelings washed over him. Julia had seemed much more relaxed over dinner, their conversation flowing easily without so much as a hint of dissension. She'd opened up about herself—her failed marriage, Steven's childhood, her love for animals and her dedication to the family veterinary practice.

In turn, he'd shared about how he'd met Tessa and their joy over Shannon's birth. He couldn't bring himself to talk much about Tessa's death, but he alluded to the pain and shock of suddenly finding himself a widower with a baby girl to raise.

There'd been moments of silence then, as if they'd each taken time to ponder their common experiences as single parents. As he reached for the canister where he kept his chocolate, he decided maybe he and Julia weren't that much different. They'd each coped as best they could with the hand God had dealt them.

The thought drew him up short. *So you're blaming God for your problems?*

Maybe before, yes. But if God really was in control, didn't He deserve gratitude for the good things, too?

The words on the plaque in the Mercy Cottage lobby flashed across his mind's eye: *Mercy unto you, and peace, and love, be multiplied.*

Truth be told, there'd been plenty of good in Lane's life. The peace he'd known on this mountain. Countless kindnesses from his friends the Vernons. The love of that little boy sleeping upstairs. His heart was opening up again, no denying it. If this was God's doing, he'd try a little harder to show his gratitude.

Julia's voice sounded behind him. "Did you get lost in there?"

Garnering his thoughts, he grabbed a chocolate bar and backed out of the pantry. "Just making sure my stash hadn't been raided."

"If I'd known it was there, it would already be long gone."

She snatched the bar from his hand and studied the label. "Fair-trade eighty percent dark. Yum. You weren't kidding around."

"Dark chocolate has many health benefits." He tried to re-claim the bar, but she skittered out of reach.

"Uh-huh, I'm sure that's the only reason you buy it."

"It's an indulgence, but I'm disciplined about it. One square a day's my limit."

"Wow." She cast him a sheepish look. "I've already admit-ted my weakness for strong coffee. You can add dark choco-late to the list now, too. Here." She reluctantly handed over the chocolate bar. "You'd better take charge of this before I abscond with it."

Chuckling, he peeled back the foil wrapper, broke off an entire row of four squares and offered it to her. "Enjoy."

"Really? Thank you!" As she savored her first bite, her eyes darkened with pleasure. "This. Is. So. Good."

"It tastes even better with coffee." He snapped one square off the next row for himself, then a second, just because. He quickly rewrapped the bar so he wouldn't be tempted to take more. Grabbing a couple of napkins along with his mug of decaf, he motioned toward the living room. "Shall we?"

He took a chance and joined her on the sofa—not so close as to intrude on her space, but near enough that if he stretched his arm across the back cushion, he might feel the silky sweep of her hair across his hand. The flickering firelight from the woodstove behind them created a cozy ambience…and maybe one that was also a tiny bit romantic? It hadn't been his inten-tion, but now he felt inclined to go with it.

Grinning, he watched her finish the last bite of chocolate. After a sip of decaf, she sighed appreciatively. "You're right, coffee and dark chocolate are the perfect pairing. I'll have to… um…" Her voice trailed off as their gazes met.

He let his fingers creep along the back of the sofa. "Have to…what?"

"I forgot what I was going to say." A nervous laugh escaped. She set down her mug and stood abruptly. "I didn't realize how late it's gotten. I should go."

"Do you have to?" He followed her across the room as she scooped up her jacket and purse. "I mean, we're actually talking for a change. It's been nice, and I was hoping you'd stay awhile."

Turning, she frowned. "A lonely mountain man makes me dinner and tops it off with chocolate and pleasant conversation in a firelit room. Where, exactly, did you assume all this was leading?"

"Whoa. Totally wrong idea." Hands raised, he took a giant step backward. "I just thought if you wanted to talk a little longer, the spare room's still made up and—"

The chime of her cell phone interrupted him. Tugging it from her purse, she gave her head a quick shake. "Sorry, I shouldn't have jumped to conclusions. It's just…it's been a long time since…" She glanced at her phone screen and went suddenly pale. "Oh, no."

He moved closer. "What's wrong? One of your patients?"

"No. My dad. He—he's in the hospital." Her breath came in shallow gasps. She fumbled with her things, nearly dropping her phone as she reached for the doorknob.

"Julia, slow down." Stepping between her and the door, he gripped her shoulders. "You're too upset to get behind the wheel. Let me drive you."

She hesitated. "But Tate—"

"I'll bundle him up. He sleeps fine in his car seat." With a firm stare, he added, "Promise me you'll wait right here while I get him."

When she gave a weak nod, he dashed upstairs. Jostling

the boy as little as possible, he got him into his hooded jacket and wrapped a blanket around him. Rowena followed them downstairs and bolted out the front door ahead of them. She seemed determined not to let Tate out of her sight, and nothing Lane said or did could coax her back in the house.

"All right, girl, if you're gonna be that way, it looks like you're riding along." He didn't know how he'd manage with the dog at the hospital, but he'd figure it out later.

All he knew was that Julia needed him, maybe for the first time since they'd met, and he had no intention of letting her down.

Chapter Nine

Letting Lane drive her to the hospital seemed a wise decision. Julia tucked her icy fingertips beneath her crossed arms and tried to focus on breathing in and out as Lane sped down I-90 into Missoula.

As soon as they reached better cellular coverage, she phoned her mother for more details. Her mom told her they'd been making supper, and her dad had gone to the pantry to put away the olive oil. The bottle had slipped from his hand and cracked, sending oil across the tiles. The next thing they knew, her dad's feet had gone out from under him. He fell against the refrigerator, banging up his hip and shoulder pretty badly, but the doctor's most pressing concern was the possibility of a concussion and brain bleed.

It was nearing nine o'clock when Lane pulled to a stop at the emergency room entrance. "I'd go in with you, but…" He tipped his head toward the back seat, where Tate snoozed. Rowena, curled up on the seat next to him, rested her chin on his leg.

"Thanks, but I'll be okay." She shrugged and quirked a smile. "Maybe the silver lining in all this is that my father will finally have to face his limitations."

He nodded. "Text or call me when you know more. We'll be waiting in the parking lot."

She'd expected to be dropped off and for Lane to head back

to the cabin. "Really, you don't have to stay." Although the fact that he'd offered warmed a tender spot in her heart. "You should get Tate home and back in his own bed."

Eyes darkening, he reached across the console to touch her arm. "I'm more worried about you."

Now she couldn't speak at all. When she found her voice, she murmured, "Then at least go over to my place. You can put Tate to bed in the portable crib." She handed him her keys. "And would you let my dogs out and put a scoop of food in their bowls? Rowena can have some, too. The canister is in the pantry."

"Sure. Don't worry about anything but looking after your dad."

Making herself open the door and get out of the truck was a thousand times harder than she'd imagined. Today, something had shifted in her relationship with Lane, and it both thrilled and terrified her. How long had it been since she'd allowed herself to be this open with anyone? To reveal her emotions with such honesty?

How long had it been since *not* being in control actually felt freeing?

She watched from beneath the portico as Lane drove away. When his taillights disappeared around the corner, she turned with a sobering breath and marched into the ER. The desk nurse buzzed her through the inner doors, and she found her mother alone in a curtained cubicle.

She gave her mother a hug. "Where's Dad?"

"More tests." Looking drained, Mom drew her toward two beige plastic chairs, and they both sat. "After I described what happened—and *why*—the doctor read your dad the riot act for not seeing our primary care physician about his symptoms long before now." She sniffed and blew her nose. "I blame myself, too. I should have been more insistent."

Julia scoffed. "How long have you been married to that guy now? Dad wrote the book on masculine mulishness." They shared a teary-eyed laugh. Serious again, Julia squeezed her mother's hand. "Has the doctor said anything yet about what could be going on with Dad?"

Mom shook her head. "That's what he's hoping the tests will reveal."

They both looked up as a nurse entered. "Just letting you know your husband is being admitted, Mrs. Frasier. They'll be taking him to his room in another half hour or so." She handed Julia's mother a slip of paper. "Here's the room number if you want to wait for him there."

"Thank you." Julia helped her mother to her feet. When Mom wavered, Julia gave her a hard look. "Did you even get to eat supper?"

"No, I guess not."

"Then let's go to the cafeteria first."

"But I couldn't—"

"You can, and you will. No matter what they find with Dad, you need to keep up your own strength."

On their way out to the corridor, Mom looped her arm through Julia's and patted her hand. "What would I do without you? You've always been the strongest one in the family."

If you only knew it's all a front! Especially tonight, when she only wanted to go home, change into her coziest robe and slipper socks, and find herself safely in the arms of the first man to burrow into her heart since those early years with her ex-husband.

The thought almost made her stumble. Her mother noticed. "Honey, are you sure *you're* all right?"

"A little tired, that's all." She gave herself a mental shake.

Because she could not—absolutely *could not*—be falling for Lane Bromley...could she?

* * *

Lane could hardly believe he was holding Julia in his arms, kissing her, being kissed in return, again and again and—

He sputtered awake to find two dachshunds prancing on his chest, their tongues going a mile a minute across his face. Next to his right ear, Rowena's hot, panting breath sounded like a locomotive.

"Hey! Knock it off, you guys." He jerked upright, sending Daisy and Dash scrambling to the other end of the sofa. Best he could recall, he'd nodded off shortly after Julia had called with an update around eleven fifteen last night.

Noticing daylight creeping through the blinds, he gave his messy hair a brisk rub. He heard Tate's whimpers coming from down the hall, the early morning, not-quite-awake kind that would soon give way to loud and forceful demands for breakfast.

No wonder the dogs had been trying to rouse him. Too bad he couldn't have lingered a little longer in that oh-so-sweet dream world.

As he brought Tate to the kitchen to scrounge up something to feed him, a knock sounded on the back door. He peeked through the curtain to see a disheveled Julia on the other side. He twisted the lock and yanked open the door.

She smiled wanly and patted Tate's cheek as she trudged inside. "Sorry if I woke everybody up. I gave you my keys."

"No problem. We were just getting breakfast." Still a bit groggy, Lane opened the fridge and then turned abruptly. "Wait. How'd you get here?"

"My mom dropped me off. She's on her way home to rest for a bit."

He studied her, concern in his eyes. "Looks like you should do the same."

"I will. But first…" She cast him a raised-brow stare. "I hope you aren't planning to give Tate *that* for breakfast."

Taking a closer look at the jar of pasta sauce he'd grabbed from the fridge, he winced and tried to cover with an excuse. "Of course not. I was just moving it out of the way."

"Mmm-hmm."

"Gampy." Tate jabbed Lane's kneecap. "I hung'y wight now!"

Julia snorted. "Gramps, why don't you let me handle breakfast? Smells like you-know-who could use a diaper change."

By the time Lane returned with a freshly diapered and even *hangrier* little boy, all three dogs had their muzzles buried in their kibble bowls, and Julia had scrambled eggs and toast on the table. The aroma of hazelnut-flavored dark roast wafted from the coffeemaker.

As he settled Tate into his booster seat, he noticed Julia's cup held an herbal tea bag. "What? You're passing on your usual morning java?"

"When we're done here, I plan to take a good, long nap. I'll get my caffeine hit after I wake up."

After filling a mug for himself, Lane joined them at the table. Spooning eggs into Tate's bowl and then onto his own plate, he asked, "How's your dad this morning?"

"He's recovering okay from the fall—no concussion, just some bruises—but the neurologist they called in is pretty sure Dad has Parkinson's."

"Oh, wow. How's he taking it?"

"Not well. I think we're all in shock."

"Julia, I'm so sorry." Lane reached toward her across the table. "But at least you have answers, and he can be treated… right?"

"Meds can mitigate the symptoms, but there's no cure." She bit her lip. "If only I'd found the courage to confront him weeks ago. If only he'd seen a doctor sooner—"

"You can't let yourself go down that road. You…you have to trust…" Lane surprised himself with what he was about to say, but against all logic, he knew it to be true. He came around the table and knelt at her side. "You have to trust that God will take care of him. That God *is* taking care of him right this very minute and has been all along."

Brow furrowed, she frowned at him. "You really believe that? But I thought…"

"And you'd have been right." He tucked a loose strand of hair behind her ear. "I'm not real sure what's happening with me in the faith department. All I do know is that years of denying God did nothing but turn me into an embittered loner. So I guess I'm ready to give Him the benefit of the doubt, and I think it might be time you should, too."

"I don't know if I can." Looking away, she shook her head. "Honestly, I'm not sure I even remember how to pray."

Tate laid down his spoon with a clatter and folded his hands. "I pway, Gammy."

Lane and Julia both gaped at the boy.

He squeezed his eyes shut and tucked his chin. "God bwess Mama and Gammy and Gampy and Gate-Gammy and Gate-Gampy and Weena and Daisy and Dash and me." Looking up with a grin, he ended with a joyful "Amen."

"Amen," Lane and Julia whispered in unison.

He looked back at her to find tears cascading down her cheeks. Moisture filled his eyes as well, and he blinked rapidly to keep the wetness from spilling over. Rising to hand her a napkin, he asked, "You okay?"

She replied with something between a nod and a shrug. Mopping her face, she glanced at Tate, who'd returned to polishing off his eggs and toast.

"Guess I shouldn't be surprised our grandson knows how to pray. His mother obviously taught him well," she murmured.

"I'm ashamed to say Shannon didn't learn it from me." He turned to fetch a handful of tissues from the box on the counter. Sharing most of them with Julia, he used one to blot his eyes and blow his nose. Back in his chair, he asked, "Was Steven a believer?"

"We stopped going to church when he was pretty young, but in college, he connected with a campus ministry." Her eyes welled again. "He tried countless times to share his faith with me, but I didn't want to hear it."

"I'm pretty sure faith doesn't come with an expiration date."

"Maybe not, but I—" A cavernous yawn interrupted her. "I'm too tired to think straight—about faith or anything else."

"I get it. I should be heading home anyway."

She gave a tiny gasp. "Oh, Lane, your livestock."

"I used your iPad to text Dan Vernon last night. Hope that was okay. He's looking after things at my place." He stood and brushed a brief kiss across her forehead. "Go on, get some rest. I'm going to stop somewhere and pick up a new phone, so you can text me later with any news about your dad. And don't worry, I'll figure out how to get your car to you."

She gave a weak nod and a smile of thanks. Before he made it out the door with Tate and Rowena, she'd traipsed down the hall to her room.

Later, with a new cell phone in his pocket, he drove past the Elk Valley mini mall and recalled the day in the grocery mart when those friends of Julia's had introduced themselves. He now regretted how aloof he'd been in response.

He still had the business card around somewhere. Maybe the Wittenbauers wouldn't mind helping him get Julia's car back to her.

Then he remembered what the man had told him that day: *I feel like the Lord's telling me you could use a friend.*

Even more so, Lane desperately needed someone he could trust with a deep conversation about God and faith.

Yes, he just might give Witt Wittenbauer a call.

"Julia Frasier!" Maddie Wittenbauer sounded well past peeved. "Why did I have to hear secondhand that your father is in the hospital?"

"It all happened so fast, and then I came home and slept for six hours." Phone on speaker in her lap, Julia absently stroked Daisy and Dash, who were stretched full-length on either side of her in the recliner. "Wait. How *did* you hear about my dad?"

"From Witt, who learned it from your mountain man. He called to ask if Witt could ride up the mountain with him and bring your car back."

"Lane called Witt?" Julia shifted abruptly, causing the dogs to squirm into more comfortable positions. "I didn't know they were acquainted."

After a moment of silence, Maddie described how she and Witt had run into Lane at the grocery mart a couple of weeks ago. "Witt had a strong sense that Lane could use a friend, so he gave him his number. He gets those feelings sometimes, you know, like a nudge from God."

A lump rose in Julia's throat. How many times in the past few months had she caught Witt looking at her with those deep-set, discerning eyes, as if he and Maddie knew a secret she didn't? A secret they'd give anything to be able to share with her if only she'd lower her guard?

Steven had acted the same way the last several times he'd been home. Maybe they all knew something she didn't. Maybe they all had a faith she could never grasp.

I'm pretty sure faith doesn't come with an expiration date, Lane had said. She was counting on that.

"Anyway," Maddie continued, "during the drive up to

Lane's, he said he needed some spiritual advice. He followed Witt to our house, and they just left to meet with Pastor Peters at the church."

If Julia had any sense—and if she didn't have a million things she should be doing in preparation for running the clinic without her dad—she'd have Maddie take her straight to the church to join them. God knew only too well how much help Julia would need to get her relationship with Him back on track.

In the meantime, maybe a long conversation with her best friend was in order. "Maddie, can you come over now?"

"I'll hop in your car and be right there. Witt can pick me up when their meeting's over."

Half an hour later, they sat at the kitchen table, Julia with a mug of coffee strong enough to kick her sluggish brain cells into gear, and Maddie with her favorite lemon-ginger tea. A plate of Maddie's homemade peanut butter cookies sat between them.

Julia nibbled on one. "I don't recall you doing much baking before you got married."

A wistful smile curled Maddie's lips. "Before Witt came into my life, I had no reason to." She wiggled a brow. "Perhaps there'll be more baking in *your* future soon?"

It was hard to miss the implication. Even harder to ignore her growing feelings for a certain mountain man. "I won't deny there's something between Lane and me, but it's too soon to know what to call it. And whatever it is, you won't find me going all Betty Crocker in the kitchen."

"Fair enough. So let's talk about what we both know is weighing heavily on your mind. I gather your dad's condition will force the retirement issue. How are you handling that?"

"Frankly, I'm at my wits' end. Interviews lately haven't been very promising, and it'll be another few weeks before the doctor we've hired will come on board. We still need an office manager, too."

Maddie touched Julia's arm. "I didn't mean just logistically. It must be hard to imagine being the only Dr. Frasier at the clinic."

Tears welled again as thoughts of Steven rose, along with all her dreams and plans for working alongside him. "Oh, Maddie, there are so many things I could—*should*—have done differently—as a daughter, a wife, a mother. Can God really forgive me for all my mistakes?"

"He already has." Maddie smiled. There was a faraway look in her eyes. "Something I've learned since first meeting Witt is that looking back should serve only three main purposes—to keep us from repeating our mistakes, to remind us how far we've come and to turn our hearts to God."

Julia scoffed. "I'm not sure I've come very far at all. But I do know I'm way past trying to make it on my own strength." She gazed at her friend through tear-filled eyes. "Can you help me find my way back to God?"

Joy sparked in Maddie's expression. She took Julia's hands in her own. "He never left you, sweetie. Just talk to Him. Tell Him what's on your heart."

It seemed both too easy and too hard. But she tried anyway. In fits and starts, she confessed the many times and ways she'd shut God out. She thanked Him for never giving up on her. She asked for the strength to relinquish control, and for the faith to turn full authority over her life to the Lord.

By the time her prayers died away, she and Maddie had both been reduced to a puddle of tears. "I know I still have a lot to work out," she said, "but I no longer feel like everything depends on me."

"That's exactly how I felt when Witt helped me find my faith again. For so many years, I prided myself in not needing anyone…until I discovered how much more beautiful life is when you're sharing it with someone who loves you." Maddie offered a knowing smile. "With someone you love in return."

"I have a feeling we're not just talking about God anymore." Julia gave her friend a hug. "I'm so happy you and Witt found each other."

Maddie gripped Julia's shoulders. "Oh, honey, we are *definitely* still talking about God. Do you think Witt and I would ever have gotten together without Him? And Lane and your sweet little grandson showing up when they did… If that isn't God's doing, I don't know what is."

She hadn't thought of it quite that way. Much as she'd come to cherish every moment she spent with Tate, when Lane first strode into her office with the news that they shared a grandson, in some ways it had felt like one more complication to work into her already too-complicated life.

And now these baffling feelings for Lane that she'd never in a million years expected. Talk about complications!

Needing space, she went to refill her coffee mug. She leaned against the counter and sipped slowly, thoughtfully. "How did you know with Witt? How'd you know it was the real thing?"

Maddie laughed. "I didn't, not at first. I only knew how he made me feel inside, how he gave me courage and made me want to hope again." Her gaze grew wistful. "Then, when we had our misunderstanding and he disappeared for a while, I didn't know how to go on. I think that's when I knew for certain, when I realized how desolate I felt without him."

Julia was definitely becoming a different person around Lane. A better version of herself, perhaps? Someone who didn't have to be perfectly in control. Someone who could enjoy a snowfall or a fireside cup of decaf or watching a boy and dog at play without continually rehashing everything she'd left undone and every problem she had yet to tackle.

Head tilted, Maddie studied her. "Why, Julia Frasier. You're falling in love."

She scoffed. "Whatever gave you that idea?"

"Because I recognize that silly smile," her friend replied with a wink and a grin. "It's the same one I see every time I happen to glance in the mirror while thinking of Witt."

Heat spread through Julia's chest and crept upward, warming her face. She'd sworn off romantic love the day she'd admitted her marriage was over. Dare she hope for a happily-ever-after this time around?

Chapter Ten

After his conversation with Witt and Pastor Peters, Lane had a lot to think about—ideas and emotions he was better off wrestling with alone for a few days. Except he missed Julia something fierce. He wanted so badly to share with her all the insights bursting in his brain and heart. But she was likely preoccupied with her father and managing the clinic, and as intense as things had gotten last weekend, a little breathing room for both of them seemed advisable.

They did text a few times. He learned her father had been released from the hospital on Tuesday and was grudgingly accepting the inevitability of retirement. In the meantime, Julia had more interviews scheduled with applicants for the office manager and associate veterinarian positions.

Which meant she couldn't break free to accompany Lane on Thursday for Tate's first visit with his mom since she'd been admitted. It was a sunny September day that had warmed quickly, even more so down in the valley. Since dogs weren't allowed inside the hospital, Dr. Yoshida arranged for them to gather on the back lawn, so Shannon could watch her active little boy at play.

Rowena served as a big furry go-between, easing some of the discomfort lingering between Lane and his daughter. Shannon's medications, though somewhat sedating, seemed to have lifted the depression slightly. It was good to hear her laughter as Tate and Rowena entertained them all with their antics. Eventually, Tate began to tucker out and crawled into Shannon's lap.

"There's my sweet boy," she murmured, snuggling him beneath her chin. She offered Lane a cautious smile. "He's growing so fast."

"He is." Lane strove for an upbeat tone. This might be his best chance to earn Shannon's approval for temporary guardianship. "He's a happy little guy, too, no trouble at all. You can see what great pals he and Rowena are."

"I just wish..." She glanced toward the building and back at Lane. "Isn't Julia coming?"

"No, honey. I told you, she's tied up at the clinic." He strove for patience in his tone. This was at least the fourth time since he'd arrived that Shannon had asked about Julia.

Swiping at an errand blond curl, she pursed her lips. "Sorry, I'm a little fuzzy-headed these days. It's my meds."

"I'm just glad you're doing better." Lane edged his lawn chair a little closer. "I... I've been praying for you, honey."

Her brow furrowed. "Really? I didn't think you..."

"Believed?" He released a self-conscious chuckle. "My faith is still about as small as the proverbial mustard seed, but I'm working on growing it."

"That's...that's good." Shannon's voice trailed off as she grew mesmerized by the swirl of hair at Tate's crown. The little guy had begun to doze in her arms.

Lane cleared his throat. "Honey, we need to talk about some stuff." When she looked up with a sleepy smile, he continued, "While you're here getting well, someone should have the legal authority to manage your financial affairs and to do whatever's necessary for Tate."

She studied him for a moment as if trying to make sense

of his words. "Oh. Yes. Dr. Yoshida said you and Julia could both be Tate's temporary guardians."

His mouth went dry. He'd informed the doctor about his findings to the contrary, but apparently Shannon hadn't understood. "Uh, no, honey, I'm afraid it can't work that way." Briefly, he explained the legalities, as well as Julia's current personal difficulties. "So—on paper, anyway—it'd just be me as Tate's guardian."

Before he'd finished speaking, he could see Shannon's resistance mounting. "No, Dad. No. It could be a long time until I—until—" Her voice was trembling now, and tears slid down her cheeks. She clutched Tate against her chest and rocked frantically. "I won't have you raising my son up there on that lonely mountain. I won't!"

Startled from his nap, Tate squirmed and began to cry. Before Lane could intervene, Rowena was pawing at Shannon's leg and pushing against her arm with her snout. The dog's actions alerted hospital staff as well, and Tate was quickly back in Lane's arms while a nurse attempted to calm Shannon.

The kid had seen his mother at her worst too many times already, and Lane decided to remove Tate from the chaos. He snatched up Rowena's leash and made for the side exit.

Someone must have summoned Dr. Yoshida, because she met him on her way out. "I take it your visit didn't end well."

"I thought you were going to help her understand about the guardianship arrangements." He couldn't hold back the irritation in his tone.

"I brought it up several times in our sessions, but I can't be sure how much she grasped." She cast Lane a sympathetic frown. "Considering her fragile state, it may be necessary for you to take other measures."

In other words, having her declared legally incapacitated. He'd hoped with all his heart it wouldn't come to that.

* * *

How did the visit go?

Julia's text showed up a few minutes after Lane had tucked Tate in bed for the night. He wished he had strong enough cell service for a voice call. Maybe if he went out to the deck…

Two whole bars showed up—a gift—so he gave it a try.

She answered right away. "Lane? Where are you?"

"At the cabin. The wind must be just right."

"You sound tired."

Gaze drifting to the starry sky, he muffled a groan. "It's been a tough day."

"Did something happen with Shannon?"

"I tried to bring up the guardianship issues, but she reacted so badly that she scared Tate, and we had to leave." He pounded a fist on the deck rail. "She didn't leave me a choice, Julia. My attorney's taking action to get her declared legally incapacitated."

"Oh, no. Are you sure she can't be reasoned with?"

"Not now. Not like this. And Dr. Yoshida won't make any predictions about how long Shannon's recovery will take. It could be several months before she's well enough to manage her own life, let alone be responsible for Tate."

Julia didn't reply right away. "You know doing this without her consent could permanently damage your relationship."

He bristled. "What else am I supposed to do?"

Her sharp exhalation sounded in his ear. "I guess this is one of those times when we're supposed to trust God, huh?"

"Guess so." The tightness in his chest eased. "I wish you could have heard Tate's bedtime prayer tonight. He asked God to make his mommy happy again and be nicer to his gampy."

Julia laughed, then murmured shyly, "I've been praying this week, too. I can't tell if God's actually listening, but talking to Him is helping me feel more hopeful."

He smiled into the night and imagined God watching from somewhere up there. "It's kind of nice to know we're dipping our toes in this faith thing together."

"I heard you went with Witt to talk with their pastor."

"So now you've got your spies checking on me?" He said it in a teasing tone.

"I told you, Maddie's my best friend. We look out for each other."

He decided to go out on a limb. "So, uh, what would you say to meeting me at their church on Sunday?"

She hesitated. "You mean for worship?"

"Sorry, too much too fast. I get it."

"No, I... I think I might actually like that."

He squeezed his eyes shut. How was it possible at his age to feel like a gawky eighth-grader who'd just asked the prettiest girl in school for a date—and she'd said yes?

"Wow. Okay. Guess I'll see you—" Static crackled. "Julia? Are you there?"

"La— Can't—"

A series of tones sounded, then nothing. He still had one bar, so he typed a quick text: Sorry, lost service.

Julia: Sorry too. Nice we could talk tho.

Lane: On for Sunday then?

Julia replied with a thumbs-up and two praying hands emojis.

Only after he went inside did he realize he hadn't asked about her father's health or things at work. They also hadn't discussed whether she'd be driving up to the cabin Saturday afternoon for what was becoming her usual extended visit with Tate.

Maybe he could change things up this weekend. Rather than

expecting her to drive an hour plus each way, he could take Tate and Rowena to her place and make dinner there. She'd had a rough week, and it would feel good to do something nice for her.

Face it, Bromley. You'd jump at any excuse to be near the woman.

Julia hoped the Lord wouldn't frown upon the fact that her overriding motivation to actually set foot in a church again was Lane, because if not for his invitation, she might have required a whole lot more convincing. True, her parents had continued their gentle nudges, which typically increased around Christmas and Easter. Eventually, she'd let them know that she was exploring her faith again. But until she made more progress, she didn't need them looking over her shoulder.

With Dad out of commission and Mom helping him adjust to his new reality, Julia had been managing the clinic mostly on her own and working late into the evening most days. On Friday, though, the ideal office manager candidate showed up like an answered prayer—*thank You, Lord!*—and Julia hired him on the spot.

On Saturday evening, seeing Lane smile across her kitchen table as she sampled his homemade lasagna was a blessed escape. He'd taken her completely by surprise with his text about bringing Tate to her house and cooking dinner. What with extending Saturday clinic hours to serve patients who'd had to be rescheduled, she couldn't possibly have made it to the cabin that afternoon.

She savored a tender bite, the tomato, cheese and basil flavors bursting across her tongue. "This is amazing."

His grin widened. "Thanks. It's another of my specialties—with credit to Lila Vernon and her pasta-making skills. And did I mention my specially seasoned elk sausage?"

"It's all delicious." Furniture making, cooking, horticulture… Was there anything this man *couldn't* do?

"Auntie Lila nice," Tate chimed in as he scooped a spoonful of mashed lasagna into his mouth.

Julia caught a morsel off his chin before it could hit the floor and become fair game for Daisy or Dash. Rowena had the good manners not to beg at the table. "I'd like to meet the Vernons one of these days. They sound like lovely people."

"They've been almost like second parents to me." Stabbing a cucumber on his salad plate, Lane softly cleared his throat. "I look forward to introducing you."

When they finished eating, Lane insisted on doing the dishes and sent Julia to the den for some one-on-one time with Tate. After they played for a bit, Julia pulled him onto her lap and picked up the storybook she'd recently come across in a box of Steven's childhood mementos. *My Little Golden Book About God* was a children's classic, and it held even more meaning for Julia now. Tate fell asleep about halfway through, but she softly read on, letting the words seep into her heart.

As she turned a page, she looked up to see Lane watching from the doorway.

"Don't stop," he said. "I want to hear the rest."

By the time she reached the end, the words had blurred. She quietly closed the book and wiped her eyes. "I'd all but forgotten how much Steven loved this book. I'm glad I saved it."

"Me, too." Coming closer, Lane smoothed back Tate's hair. "Guess I should get this little guy home. I still have evening chores to do."

Julia helped him slip Tate's arms into his tiny gray fleece jacket and walked them to the door. "Thanks again for dinner. It… It meant a lot."

"To me, too." Stepping onto the porch, he turned, his eyes darkening. "Julia, I—"

Tate lifted his head and whimpered. "Mama?"

"Go back to sleep, Tater Tot." Lane soothed him with a pat while casting Julia a regretful frown. "We'd better go."

And just when she'd thought Lane might kiss her good-night. She held back a sigh. "See you at church in the morning?"

"We'll be there." He snickered as he glanced down at Rowena. "All of us, most likely, since these two are practically inseparable."

"You've met Witt's dog, Ranger, so you know it won't be a problem."

She watched Lane drive away and then closed the door to find Daisy and Dash glaring up at her as if it was all her fault their giant playmate had left. If she'd known how well the three of them would get along, she might not have worked so hard to convince Lane to take Rowena. Still, she had no regrets. Tate and "Weena" would be lifelong companions.

It was only a little past seven o'clock, but with fatigue taking its toll, she was ready to fall into bed.

Before she made it down the hall, her phone rang. It was her mother, sounding overwrought. "Honey, we need some help. Can you come right over?"

She arrived at her parents' house to find her father collapsed on the living room floor and without the physical strength to get himself up. But would the prideful, stubborn man let Mom call 9-1-1, or even ask their brawny next-door neighbor for assistance? Not a chance.

That left it up to Julia and her mother to wrestle him into the recliner. Julia wouldn't leave until he'd rested and regained some muscle control. With threats and negotiations, they persuaded him to use the walker he despised so they could help him to the bedroom. It was almost midnight by then, and Julia was ready to collapse.

"You can't continue taking care of him alone, Mom." Julia gathered her things. "Not as fast as the Parkinson's is progressing."

Looking drained, Mom pressed a hand to her forehead. "I know, I know. We're still figuring this out."

"Well, don't take too long, or you'll only destroy your own health."

"And what about yours?" Her mother's lips thinned in a concerned frown. "I feel awful about the burden all this has placed on you at the clinic."

"I'm managing. Amy and Dylan are helping to pick up the slack." She wouldn't mention losing a few patients to other veterinary practices. If too many more jumped ship, she wouldn't need to worry about hiring a third veterinarian. They might even have to let a couple of their part-time techs go.

At the door, Mom drew her into a hug. "If your dad's illness is teaching me anything, it's that there are more important things in life than keeping the family business going. If and when you feel it's time to let the practice go, so be it."

Julia pulled away with a gasp. "Mom, no—"

"I mean it, honey. You have a grandson now, Steven's precious little boy." Sniffling, she found a tissue in her pocket and dabbed her cheeks. "Don't let a false sense of obligation deprive you of the time you could be spending with him."

"But I love the clinic. I'm proud of what we do there. I'm proud every time I glimpse the Frasier name on the front door."

"Of course you are." Mom motioned in the direction of the bedroom. Voice breaking, she went on, "But you see what it's cost your father—cost all of us. Whatever decisions you make, be sure they're for the right reasons."

The next morning, Julia was sleeping more soundly than she had in weeks. Only Daisy's and Dash's strident barks, combined with the two of them leaping back and forth across her on the bed, finally roused her. And no wonder they were so anxious—the bedside clock read 10:34.

"Okay, okay, kiddos." She grabbed her robe and jammed her feet into slippers. "Outside first, and then I'll get your breakfast."

From another part of the house came the muffled ring of her cell phone. Hoping it wasn't Mom with another urgent Dad problem, she jostled her foggy brain into remembering where she'd dropped her things after getting home last night. She traced the sound to the pocket of the hoodie she'd worn and answered without looking at the display.

"Julia?" Lane's voice. Praise music played in the background. "Did you change your mind?"

She slammed a palm to her forehead. "I'm so sorry. I never set my alarm." Explaining about rushing over to help her parents last night, she apologized again.

"Don't worry about it. I understand." Other voices sounded close by. Lane excused himself for a moment, and Julia heard him speaking to someone else. Then he came back on the line. "Maddie wants to talk to you. I'm putting her on."

"Hey, Jules. You take it easy, okay? I'll bring a meal over later."

"You don't have to do that. Really, I'm fine."

"No, you're not, so don't argue. I'm hanging up now. Bye!"

The last thing Julia heard before the line went silent was Tate's excited "Yay! Dis Jesus house!"

If not for the dancing dachshunds at her feet, she'd have plopped into the nearest chair and sobbed out her shame and disappointment. She used to believe she was a lot stronger than this, but tears came too easily these days. "I'm sorry about church, God," she whispered with a skyward glance as she opened the back door for the dogs. "Do good intentions count?"

Later, fortified by two large mugs of extra-strong dark roast, she tossed in a load of laundry and sat down at the kitchen table with her laptop to check email and pay bills.

She was just finishing when Daisy and Dash broke out in excited yips and raced for the front door two whole seconds before the doorbell rang. She marched to the foyer and maneuvered past them.

A peek through the peephole revealed the source of their anticipation. Rowena and Ranger were both sniffing at the other side of the door. Witt, Maddie, Lane and Tate waited on the porch behind the dogs.

Knowing she'd never win at holding her pups back, she stepped out of the way before opening the door. The four canines greeted one another with a lot of sniffing and prancing, and somehow, the four adult humans managed to herd the dogs to the backyard.

Once the house was semi-quiet again, Julia turned to the others. "You guys! What are you doing here?"

"I told you I'd bring a meal." Maddie set two large brown restaurant bags on the kitchen counter. "After church, we stopped by the Smith Family Hometown Café and ordered takeout."

Aromas were already teasing Julia's senses. "Does one of those bags happen to contain my favorite chicken potpie?"

"Of course." Maddie was already pulling plates from Julia's cupboard. "We thought we'd join you, if that's okay."

How could she say no to her thoughtful and generous friend? "That'd be great."

While Maddie and Witt set out the food, Julia stepped outside to where Lane was keeping a close eye on Tate as he romped with the dogs.

He offered a tentative smile. "Sorry if we intruded on your plans for a quiet afternoon."

"It's fine. And I still feel awful about standing you up this morning. I'd really wanted to be there—*needed* to be there." Here came those annoying tears again. She sniffed and swallowed.

"So we'll try again next week." Lane's fingers brushed hers, and she let her hand slide into his. So warm, so reassuring, so…*right*.

In the yard, the little dogs were weaving through the big dogs' legs while a giggling Tate tried to do the same. Rowena was tall enough that he barely had to stoop. Ranger's legs weren't nearly as long, so Tate dropped to his hands and knees.

Laughing out loud, Lane pulled his phone from his pocket. "I need to video this to show Shannon."

"She'll love it." Julia chuckled as he recorded several seconds of dog-and-toddler mayhem. When he lowered his phone, she asked, "Are you still going through with having Shannon declared incapacitated?"

"It's in the works. Under the circumstances, my attorney thinks he can get a judge to act on it pretty quickly." He grimaced. "I know you have reservations. I do, too, but it's the only way to ensure my right to make decisions on their behalf."

Before Julia could respond, the back door opened. "Lunch is on the table," Maddie called. "Come get it while it's hot."

Lane tucked away his phone. "Let's go eat, Tater Tot."

"Not before you wash your hands, little guy." Julia ushered him inside and down the hall to the bathroom.

On the way, she couldn't help recalling the first time she'd met Shannon, nor the young mother's desperate plea for Julia to make sure Tate wouldn't spend his childhood on the mountain.

Yes, Lane's place was remote. But the more time Julia spent there, the more at peace she felt. The clean air, the breathtaking views, the sense of time slowing down and the real world melting away… She'd come to cherish her trips up to the cabin. After the week she'd just had, she needed that sense of tranquility all the more.

She needed Lane.

Who was she kidding? Despite what her mother had said, she did feel a responsibility to the family business. And she did love her work. Not to mention, her parents would need her more than ever now. And Steven's death had certainly taught her the utter futility of imagining a perfect future.

God, if You're really listening, give me strength for today and help me trust the future to You.

Chapter Eleven

Dr. Yoshida had given the okay for Lane to bring Tate and Rowena for another visit. Lane almost wished he could come up with an excuse not to go. He didn't know how his daughter would react when she learned a judge had granted him emergency temporary guardianship of Tate while his petitions were further examined.

He didn't know how to help her understand that even though he'd made mistakes, his deepest motivation had always been love.

He arrived at Mercy Cottage on Thursday around midmorning. Tate was much more energetic this time of day, but he'd start getting hungry closer to noon, which would give Lane an easy out if things with Shannon got uncomfortable.

Hopefully by now, Dr. Yoshida had reassured her that the legal arrangements he'd made were for the best and would remain in place only until she'd recovered. He sent up yet another prayer—unpracticed as he was—asking the Lord not only to soften his daughter's heart toward him, but to grant her healing in mind and spirit.

The visit began well, with Shannon seeming more clearheaded. They chatted for a few minutes about inconsequential things, and then Tate needed a diaper change. Before taking the boy inside to the visitors' restroom, Lane left his phone with Shannon so she could watch the video of Tate playing with the four dogs in Julia's backyard.

When he returned, he suggested they take a walk around the grounds so Tate could burn off some energy. Gripping Rowena's leash, the boy trotted ahead. Along the way, Shannon slowed to pick up a bronze-tinted leaf. As she studied it with a pensive frown, Lane took the opportunity to ease into the subject he'd been dreading.

His daughter surprised him with her quick assent. "I get it, Dad. No need to explain." She twirled the leaf stem between her fingers. "I'll sign whatever papers you need me to."

"That's... That's great." Relief swept through him at not having to pursue the "legally incapacitated" route after all. "I promise, honey, this is only temporary."

She smiled and nodded. "Tate, sweetie, wait for Mommy!"

Wow. Maybe he should simply be thankful and move on, but...had this been a tiny bit *too* easy?

Before leaving later, he asked for a moment of Dr. Yoshida's time. She met him on the front sidewalk after he'd settled Tate and the dog in the truck. "Are you sure Shannon's okay with everything?"

"She understands the importance of ensuring her own as well as her son's welfare. In fact, I'm so encouraged by her overall improvement that I'm considering an overnight furlough soon. It would be good for Shannon to spend quality time with her little boy away from the hospital. Would you be up for that?"

"Definitely."

Anxious to share the news with Julia, he headed to the veterinary clinic in hopes of catching her between patients. He figured she'd probably work through lunch, so he stopped on the way to pick up a burger, a grilled chicken salad and a kids' meal. He wasn't averse to locking her in her office if it would force her to take five minutes to sit down and eat something.

As soon as he walked in the door, a young woman in purple scrubs burst from behind the counter. Over her shoulder, she called, "Rowena's here!"

Soon she was joined by two more vet techs. All of them fawned over the big dog, who was literally lapping up the attention.

Julia entered from the corridor. "I wondered what all the commotion was about."

"Gammy!" Tate ran to her, arms upraised for her to hold him.

"Hi there, sweetheart." Lifting him onto her hip, she cast Lane a curious grin. "This is a nice surprise."

He held up the fast-food bag. "I brought lunch. Can I steal you away for a few minutes?"

"Go on, Dr. J," the purple-clad tech said. "We've got things covered."

"Thanks, Amy. Why don't you take Rowena to the back and get her vitals? I'll give her a quick exam while she's here."

In Julia's office, Lane set out the food he'd brought, only to have Julia snatch up the burger he'd intended for himself. Guess he'd have to settle for the chicken salad. He pulled a chair closer, balancing Tate on one knee while the kid scarfed down grilled chicken nuggets and ignored the fruit cup.

Between bites, Lane described his visit with Shannon. "If I weren't so relieved, I'd be suspicious."

"Your daughter's improving. Maybe just accept it for the good news it is." Julia dabbed mustard from the corner of her mouth before taking a sip of diet cola. "So what happens next?"

"On the way over, I called Harry, my lawyer. He's finalizing the details."

Smiling, Julia took another monstrous bite from the hamburger. Seemed she had every intention of keeping this a five-minute lunch break. After another swig of cola, she shoved her chair back. "Stay here and finish. Sorry, but I've got to get back to my patients. And thanks again for lunch. Now I may actually survive the afternoon."

"Julia—"

"Oh, yes, Rowena. I'll have Amy bring her to you as soon as we're done." The door banged shut behind her.

Tate looked up with a frown. "Gammy go bye-bye?"

"Grammy's a busy lady."

Should Lane be suspicious of her, too? Her texts since last Sunday had taken on a different tone. Less chatty, more... What else could he call it but polite? And just when he'd thought something meaningful was happening between them. He'd like to believe she was merely preoccupied. Who could blame her, what with all the complications she was dealing with?

He only hoped her work stress would ease off soon, because with every minute he spent with her, he grew increasingly certain he wanted to be much more to Julia Frasier than Tate's other grandparent.

Until she'd caught a whiff of the juicy burger Lane had brought, Julia hadn't realized how hungry she was.

Now the meal sat like a rock in her stomach. She'd gulped it down entirely too quickly, partly because she really did need to stay on schedule today, but also because she was afraid if she spent too much time in Lane's presence, her resolve to slow things down between them would wither.

Yes, her attempt to stop trying to control everything was failing miserably. But these feelings for Lane seemed like the one thing she most needed to keep under control. Otherwise, she risked losing her focus—which in turn could mean losing the clinic she and her parents had invested so much of themselves in.

Her examination of Rowena proved the big dog healthy in every respect. Her injured leg was mending well. Julia had Amy return the dog to Lane, and she made sure to be in an exam room with a patient when they left.

Later that afternoon, she had a Zoom interview with another candidate for associate veterinarian. Nikki Ramirez, three years out of veterinary college, was currently on staff at a twenty-four-hour emergency vet clinic but wanted a position with regular daytime hours. The young woman was personable, came with solid references and could start the end of next week. Julia scheduled an in-person interview and clinic tour on Saturday afternoon.

Which meant she'd once again leave work too late to make the drive up to Lane's cabin. She texted him Friday evening to let him know.

Good news and bad news, I guess? he replied. How about trying church again on Sunday?

That was something she'd told herself she needed to do no matter what. Definitely. This time I'll set TWO alarms.

The Saturday interview went well, and before the young doctor left, they'd inked an employment contract. A go-getter new office manager who was already proving his worth, two impressive new vets soon to join the staff—was she finally seeing light at the end of this particular tunnel? For the first time in too long to remember, the chronic tension between her shoulder blades had begun to ease.

The world looked even brighter Sunday morning after her best night's sleep in ages. She made it to Elk Valley Community of Faith with ten minutes to spare.

Maddie and Witt arrived at almost the same time. Maddie rushed over to give Julia a welcoming hug. "You made it. I'm so glad."

Julia snorted a self-deprecating laugh. "After how this week turned out, I thought God deserved a proper thank-you." On their way to the building, she told her friend about filling all the staff positions. "I'll soon be able to slow down and hopefully spend more time with my grandson."

"And a certain ruggedly handsome mountain man, too?" Maddie winked, then looked over her shoulder as a big maroon truck turned into the parking area. "Speaking of whom…"

Julia's stomach twisted. "Please, you're jumping to conclusions. Lane and I are just—"

"Don't you dare say *just friends*." Maddie speared her with an icy turquoise stare, though her tone was tender. "Have you forgotten how long we've known each other? Your feelings for this man are written all over your face."

She glanced past Maddie to see Lane ambling their way with Tate propped on his hip. Rowena tugged on the leash in her excitement to greet Ranger. Maybe she should have stayed home after all, because she could read in Lane's warm smile and the hopeful look in his eyes exactly how much he was beginning to care for her.

"Gammy!" Tate practically flew from Lane's arms into hers.

Huffing a startled laugh, she caught her balance. "Careful there, fella."

Lane steadied them both. "He kept asking me all the way here if you were really coming today. How'd the interview go?"

"Great. We're now fully staffed—or will be, once everyone reports in."

"So just a couple more weeks?" His words ended on an expectant note.

"Yes, a couple more weeks." Behind her, the church doors opened, releasing a burst of praise music. "We should go find seats." Preferably near the back, and not right next to Lane. Her feelings for him remained a bit too complex for comfort.

Having a squirming Tate planted between them helped minimally. Julia chuckled to herself when she noticed the dogs had better church manners, both of them stretched out between the pews for naps.

In fact, it appeared Witt and Ranger had started a trend. Julia counted at least six other canines of various sizes and breeds among the congregants. The sight wrapped around her heart like a warm, fuzzy sweater.

It could have been the dogs, or it could have been the pastor's message based on the New Testament scripture about "the peace of God, which passeth all understanding"—or more likely both—but when Julia stepped out into the midday sun an hour later, her spirit felt ten times lighter. She would have asked God where He'd been the last twenty-plus years, but she already knew the answer. He'd been right there with her the whole time, if only her eyes of faith had been open to see.

Maddie and Witt had taken charge of Tate and the dogs, leaving Julia to follow behind with Lane. He leaned toward her ear. "You look happier than I've seen you recently."

A shiver went through her. She cast him an appraising smile. "I could say the same about you."

"It's been an encouraging week in many ways." His voice softened. "Any chance that opens the door a little wider for... us?"

She didn't answer right away—she *couldn't*, considering the staccato drumming of her heart. After a hard swallow, she murmured, "Ask me again in a week or two, okay?"

His mouth flattened into a smug smile. "I'll do that."

Guess he couldn't blame her for leaving their relationship in limbo for the time being. After how quickly Julia had scurried out of her office on Thursday, Lane had fretted all the way back home that she'd both literally and figuratively closed the door on him.

Today, though, he sensed her heart inching open again, and it made him ridiculously giddy—a fact he had to work extra hard to conceal.

Since she'd been tied up all day yesterday, he'd hoped she'd be free to spend this afternoon with him and Tate.

"I wish I could," she told him as they stood beside her SUV. "But my mom has been looking after my dad almost 24/7 since he came home from the hospital, and I promised her I'd stay with him for a few hours today so she could have some time to herself."

"Tate and I could join you," Lane offered. "A visit with his great-grandson could be good for your dad."

Julia scrunched her brows together. "It's a little too soon, I think. Dad is still coming to terms with his diagnosis, plus adjusting to new meds, and Mom says he hasn't been very pleasant to be around."

"Another time, then." Moving a step closer, he took her hand and felt her shiver. "I'm here for you, Julia. And while you're consumed with running the clinic and helping your parents, don't neglect taking care of *you*."

The emotion in her eyes when she looked up at him spoke of long-ago hurt and stifled hope. It made him wonder what kind of a creep she'd once been married to that had made her believe she could rely on no one but herself.

When she glanced away, he gently cupped her cheek and turned her face toward his. "I mean it, Julia. You can count on me. Always."

"Gampy!" came Tate's impatient shout. He'd been walking Rowena on the lawn with Witt, Maddie and Ranger. "Go now!"

Lane chuckled softly. "Somebody wants lunch. Guess I should be going."

"Guess so." A tiny smile curled Julia's lips as she covered his hand with her own. "Thank you. Your... Your friendship means more than I can say."

Was it only wishful thinking, or had she imbued that ordinary term *friendship* with something more? It might be too soon to call what they had a *relationship*, romantically speaking, but he hoped with all his heart they were headed that way.

Over the next couple of weeks, the texts from Julia began sounding more positive. She really liked the office manager she'd hired, and now that one of the new veterinarians had joined the staff, her workload was easing.

On the downside, her father had been complicating things by insisting on a supervisory role at the clinic. She explained that she could hardly tell him no, since it would be depriving him of what little dignity and sense of purpose he had left.

Lane could understand. He saw something similar during his regular Thursday visits with Shannon. Each week, when Tate rushed headlong into her arms with a loud "Miss you, Mama!" a spark of life lit her eyes, as if being needed by her little son were all the medicine she required just then. Even so, Dr. Yoshida reported there continued to be difficult days, when grief and sadness took Shannon to places so dark and remote that no one seemed able to reach her.

Fall temperatures continued their downward trend. Since Rowena wasn't allowed inside at Mercy Cottage, Lane left the dog at the cabin when he took Tate to visit Shannon the first Thursday in October. Tate wasn't happy about leaving his doggy pal behind, but when his mother cheerfully joined him on the floor with crayons and drawing paper, the boy was soon busily sketching line-and-circle figures he claimed were Lane, Shannon, Rowena and himself.

Then Tate proudly announced one of his unrecognizable drawings was "Gammy." There was even something vaguely resembling a stethoscope around what Lane assumed was the figure's neck. Laughing, Lane decided Julia should see it. He gave her a call as he was leaving.

"I know it's last minute," he said, "but any chance you could break free to meet us for lunch?"

"You know what? I think I can actually say yes." She gave a lighthearted laugh, a sound he'd rarely heard from her, and it made his own heart lift.

"That's great. Name a place close to your clinic, and we'll meet you there."

Half an hour later, they were seated in a booth at a pub-style sandwich shop, Lane and Julia across from each other, and Tate in a tall wooden booster chair pushed up to the open end of the table. While they waited for their order, Lane unfolded Tate's drawing and pushed it across to Julia.

"Oh, yes, that's definitely me," she said with mock serious-ness. "See? There's my bedhead first thing in the morning, and my frazzled brain leaking out, and my long, *long* arms—" she stretched them to encircle Tate "—so that I can give my Tater Tot even bigger hugs!"

He giggled and squirmed. "Gammy, no tickle me!"

The server brought their orders, and conversation ebbed while Lane got Tate situated with his triangle-cut grilled cheese sandwich and orange wedges.

After a bite of her chicken club, Julia asked, "So the visit with Shannon went well?"

"It did. She really looks forward to spending time with Tate every week. She's hoping you can visit again soon, too."

"Now that my life is settling down a bit, I plan to." She sipped her iced tea. "And the legal stuff? Still no pushback?"

"None at all. Papers are signed and on the way to being finalized." Frowning, Lane gave his head a brisk shake. "To be honest, I'm kind of in shock. I never expected Shannon would be this agreeable."

"It has to be a positive sign, don't you think?"

"I want to believe so, but…something feels off about it." He gnawed off a mouthful of his Reuben and then had to mop sauerkraut off his chin.

"Surely she's not just pretending to go along with the arrangements? What would be the point?"

"True." Lane gave a rueful laugh. "If I really am at the point of trusting God with all this, then I ought to quit overthinking Shannon's reaction and just be grateful."

"Easier said than done, as I know all too well." Helping Tate get a better grip on his sippy cup, Julia cast Lane a sideways glance. "Don't ask me how I'm doing with putting my parents in the Lord's hands. It's taking a conscious effort every day."

"At least we're trying, which—for me, anyway—is a marvel in and of itself."

Julia smirked. "A month ago, I'd have said nothing short of a wedding or a funeral would get me back inside a church." She paused, a faraway look in her eyes. "Maybe people like us need to reach the end of our own strength before we can admit how desperately we need God."

They fell into a thoughtful silence and continued eating, chuckling now and then over something silly Tate did with his food. The kid was learning all the right moves to divert his grandparents' attention and get them to smile.

After finishing her sandwich, Julia checked her watch and let out a gasp. "I totally lost track of time. I have to get back to the clinic." Scooting out of the booth, she pulled her wallet from her purse and began tugging out bills. "Here, this should cover—"

"Put your money away." Lane stuffed the cash back into her hand, his fingers closing around her fist. "I invited you. This is my treat."

"But—"

"We promised to cut back on the arguments, remember? So consider this your chance to practice." He winked. "Give me five seconds—or maybe ten—to get the munchkin cleaned up, and we'll walk out with you."

His estimate was on the low side for wiping Tate's face and hands and working that wiggly little body into a jacket. Julia's tense posture said she was anxious to be on her way, but she waited by the door while Lane paid their bill. As they walked out, she muttered a reluctant thank-you.

Fingers closing around her elbow, he compelled her to face him. "Be honest with me, Julia. Was my treating you to lunch so hard for you because you'd rather not feel obligated, or because it felt too much like a date?"

"I… I don't know." She grimaced. "Both, I suppose."

"Well, how about I clarify the situation once and for all?" Shifting Tate to his other hip, he slid his free hand beneath her ponytail. Gently but firmly, he pulled her to him for a kiss he hoped would leave no doubt as to his deepening feelings.

"Oh, my…" A smile teased up the corners of her lips. Her stunned stare reminded him of the glassy-eyed mule deer he'd caught in his headlights the other night.

Tate chortled. "Gampy kiss Gammy! Again, do again!"

Hands lifted, she put more space between them and released a shaky laugh. "How am I supposed to blithely move through the rest of my workday after *that*?"

Her discomfiture pleased Lane in ways he couldn't even describe. "I'm sure you'll find a way."

Chapter Twelve

When Julia returned to work after lunch, she found her father holding court in the clinic kitchen. Apparently, he'd been regaling any available staff member with stories of his early years as a veterinarian.

Sidling into the room, Julia was relieved to see Dad's fancy new walker beside his chair. He'd been embarrassed about using it at first, but Mom had insisted early on—either he agreed to faithfully use his walker, or she wouldn't let him leave the house.

Julia's mother skirted the two junior techs taking their lunch break and joined her at the door.

"He's winding down, I think," Mom said. "Then I'll…" Her voice trailed off as she studied Julia with a furrowed brow. "Honey, you're positively *glowing.*"

"What? No!" Turning away slightly, she gave her head a brisk shake.

"Don't pretend with me. I know you met Lane for lunch. Did he…" She gasped and dropped her tone to a whisper. "Did he kiss you?"

Julia scurried into the corridor. One hand pressed to the side of her rapidly warming face, she collapsed against the wall.

Her mother followed, a gleeful grin brightening her eyes. "He did! Oh, honey, I'm so happy for you."

"Stop, Mom." She gripped her mother's fluttering hands. "It's all too new, and I'm not sure I'm ready for—for—"

"For falling in love? My dearest daughter—"

"Your *only* daughter."

"Which means I cherish you all the more. You've waited so long to put yourself first. Isn't it about time?"

Just then, Amy peeked out of an exam room. "Your next patient's waiting, Dr. J."

"Be right there." With a forced smile, she ducked into her office to grab her lab coat.

She hadn't known how to answer her mother's question. Or maybe she was afraid she'd been putting herself first all along. This wall she'd erected around her heart, her efforts to control every situation—weren't those merely a form of selfishness?

Somehow she made it through the afternoon. Several routine appointments plus an emergency procedure to suture a dog's ear after a tussle with his housemate helped to distract her from thoughts of Lane and that amazing—and extremely persuasive—kiss.

Catching up with desk work after closing time, she reviewed the next day's schedule. Her first appointment wasn't until 9:45, and Dr. Ramirez could cover any early walk-ins. This might be her best chance to see Shannon.

First thing Friday morning, she phoned Mercy Cottage to ask if she could visit. A few minutes later, Dr. Yoshida's secretary called back with a yes. She drove right over and was escorted to Shannon's room.

The young woman greeted her with a hug. "When they told me you were coming again, I could hardly wait."

"I meant to visit sooner, but work's been so hectic." Julia's smile warmed as she smoothed back one of Shannon's blond curls. "You look like you're feeling a little better."

"I'm trying—really, really trying." Taking Julia's hand,

Shannon drew her toward a small table and chairs by the window. As they sat, she continued, "I have to get well for Tate. And that's the main reason I've been wanting to see you so badly."

A warning twinge tightened Julia's stomach. "If you're having reservations about your dad's guardianship…"

"I know it's for the best right now." Shannon waved dismissively. "Let's talk about something else. Do you have any new photos of Tate?"

They spent a few minutes flipping through the photos on Julia's phone, and then Julia asked how Shannon's week had been.

Anticipation lit the girl's eyes. "Did you know I'll be getting a furlough soon?"

"Your dad mentioned you might be allowed to spend a weekend at home with Tate. That sounds wonderful."

"There's just one problem." Shannon's lower lip trembled. "I… I don't think I can face going back to my dad's cabin."

Julia reached across the table to cover Shannon's hand. "I understand it was hard for you growing up there, but it'll be different now. Besides, it's so peaceful in the mountains, so… healing. Every time I'm there, it's like the cares of my everyday world melt away."

She wouldn't mention that being near Lane in his element sparked a whole different kind of tension.

Heaving a frustrated sigh, Shannon turned her gaze toward the window. "I can't. There are too many bad memories."

"But your dad loves you so much. Let this be a time to make new memories—happier memories."

"I'm just not ready yet." Shannon sniffled and swiped at a tear. She cast Julia a pleading look. "But if you'd let me stay with you…"

"For your furlough weekend?" Julia wasn't sure how Lane

would take to the idea, but it could be a viable compromise. "It's a possibility, but—"

Shannon nearly toppled the table in her rush to wrap her arms around Julia. "Thank you! I've been praying so hard about this, and I knew I could count on you."

"Okay, honey, okay." Julia tamped down a nagging sense of unease as she gently guided Shannon back to her chair. The girl seemed a little too jubilant over the whole idea. "We'll need to clear this with your doctor first."

"I'm sure she'll be fine with it. So you'll arrange with my dad to have Tate at your house for the weekend, right?"

"Yes—again, with Dr. Yoshida's approval." She checked the time, almost relieved she had to be on her way. Rising, she gathered her coat and purse. "I need to get to work, honey, but I promise I'll look into this."

Between appointments later, she phoned Mercy Cottage and requested a callback from Dr. Yoshida. The doctor returned her call as she was finishing up for the day.

After supplying the gist of her conversation with Shannon, she went on, "It isn't that I wouldn't love to have her stay with me for a weekend. I'm just concerned she's using me as an excuse to avoid facing her issues with her father."

"Highly likely," the doctor acknowledged. "We're continuing to work through those issues in therapy, but in the meantime, I still believe it would be extremely beneficial for her to have some time with her son away from the hospital. If you're agreeable, I'd like to plan for a week from this Saturday. It would be just one night, and you would need to commit to staying with her the entire time."

Julia consulted her calendar. By then, Dr. Kruger would have joined the practice and they'd be fully staffed. If any questions arose, she could always be reached by phone.

"I'm sure that can be arranged," she said. "I'll do anything I can to help in Shannon's recovery."

"You *what*?" Lane nearly dropped an armful of logs on his toe. Good thing Julia had kept Tate and Rowena well away from the woodshed opening.

"Shannon's doctor agreed to the idea." Her nose and cheeks were red from the cold, but the determination in her eyes shone like embers.

After stacking more logs in the utility wagon, he started hauling it through the snow toward the cabin. Yes, he could see the logic of not bringing Shannon to the mountain for her first overnight away from the hospital, but it hurt nonetheless. He wanted to make amends with his daughter, and since the home where he'd raised her was their only tangible point of connection, how else could he hope to reach her?

"Go Mama?" Tate said.

"Not today, sweetie. Lane, wait up." Julia grunted like she'd just lifted something heavy—Tate, no doubt—and her steps crunched behind his.

Without looking back, he hefted an armful of logs and marched up the deck steps. It would be a frigid night with more snow predicted, so he needed to fill his firewood rack with enough to last through the weekend.

"Lane." Julia was breathing hard as she reached the top step.

He dusted his gloved hands and rolled his shoulders before turning toward her. "Shut the gate, please."

"I *know*." Her glare could have melted the icicles off the eaves. With precise movements, she closed the thigh-high gate Lane had installed to bar Tate's access to the deck stairs. After testing the latch with a quick shake, she set Tate down.

Lips in a twist, Tate moved between them and held up his

hands like a referee in a boxing match. "Gammy Gampy no fight!"

Rowena gave a punctuating bark.

Julia rolled her eyes. "Truce?"

"Truce." Lane marched to the cabin door and held it open while the woman, boy and dog trooped inside. After stripping off his jacket and gloves, he helped Tate out of his winter things, took Julia's coat from her and draped everything on hooks behind the door.

In the meantime, the aroma of brewing coffee enticed Julia to the kitchen. As soon as she'd texted she was heading his way, he'd set the coffeemaker to start exactly one hour later. He knew all too well how she loved her fully caffeinated dark roast.

Leaving Tate and Rowena playing ball on the living room carpet, he joined Julia at the counter and filled a mug for himself. "I shouldn't have jumped down your throat like that."

"And I could have used a bit more tact when I broke the news."

"Well, you did sound a wee bit smug about the whole thing."

She carried her mug to the table and sank into a chair. "I didn't mean to, honestly."

Taking the chair kitty-corner from hers, he set down his coffee and reached for her hands. Soft and fine-boned, they were warm from cradling her mug and fit so comfortably into his work-roughened grip. He grew so entranced holding her hands that for a moment, he forgot what they'd been talking about.

"I'm really sorry," she murmured. "I know how much it would mean to you to have Shannon home again. Maybe by her next furlough, she'll be ready."

Tate traipsed into the kitchen, his wise-beyond-his-years glance darting between them. "Gammy Gampy aw better?"

"Yes," Lane assured. "Grammy and Grampy are all better."

Arms akimbo, the boy nodded and grinned. "Otay, den. Kiss."

Heat shot up Lane's neck. Forcing a swallow, he lifted his gaze to Julia's. "Would that be okay with you?"

Mischief lit her eyes. "Can we dare risk disobeying a direct order?"

"That would be extremely dangerous, in my opinion." He stood, then pulled her to him and planted a whopper of a kiss on her surprised lips.

"Yay!" Tate clapped his hands and laughed. "Yay, yay, yay!"

Ending the kiss, Lane felt like celebrating, too. He grinned down at Julia and savored her languidly happy expression. "If all our arguments could end like this, I'd be picking fights with you every hour on the hour."

"Actually, I'd prefer to skip the arguing and get straight to the making-up part." She interlaced her fingers behind his neck and tilted her head, clearly waiting for another kiss.

He wouldn't let the moment slip by.

Lane had resigned himself to the fact that Shannon would spend the weekend at Julia's house. However, since he'd be making the trip into town anyway to bring Tate to Julia's, he made arrangements with the Mercy Cottage staff to pick up his daughter on the way.

Shortly before eight o'clock on Saturday morning, he loaded Tate and Rowena into the truck along with enough clothing, diapers and dog food to last until Sunday evening. Shannon was packed and ready to go when he arrived. Dr. Yoshida escorted her out to the truck, and while she climbed in and got situated, the doctor handed Lane a zippered pouch containing Shannon's meds and a page of instructions.

"It's very important for Shannon to have her medications on schedule," the doctor said, "so be sure you and Julia are both clear about everything on the information sheet. My cell phone number is included, and I can be reached all weekend, day or night. If for any reason you cannot get through to me, call the Mercy Cottage emergency number."

The urgency in her tone made him feel slightly panicky. "Is there any reason to think something could go wrong?"

"No, I'm only being thorough." Smiling, Dr. Yoshida gave his arm a reassuring pat. "I've been preparing Shannon for today, and she's ready. She also understands she needs to maintain her routine and rest when she needs to. With proper supervision and the love of her family, this should be a positive experience all around."

What else could he do but trust the doctor? Thanking her, he tucked the pouch into his coat pocket and got in behind the wheel.

Shannon had been leaning between the seats to play patty-cake with a giggling Tate. She swiveled and fastened her seat belt. "I'm ready. Let's go."

He tried not to be overly concerned about the almost manic glint in her eyes. Why shouldn't she be excited about her first foray into normal life since he'd checked her in to the hospital?

Julia was watching for them from her front porch and strode out to the truck as soon as he parked in her driveway. While she helped Shannon get Tate and the dog from the back seat, Lane hefted the luggage and pet supplies. Following the women inside, he felt pretty much like an afterthought. When Rowena looked back from the porch as if waiting for him, he wanted to believe the dog actually cared about his feelings, but more than likely, she only wanted to make sure he hadn't forgotten her bag of kibble.

Inside, Julia relieved him of the dog supplies and directed him to the guest room with Shannon's and Tate's things. When he returned, he found everyone in the den. Shannon sat on the floor with Tate on her lap, both laughing while the dachshunds entertained them with a game of tug-of-war. Rowena seemed to understand she was too big and ungainly to join in. Instead, she parked herself as close as she could get to Tate without being in the way.

Julia came over to stand by Lane. "They're having a great time already. Just look at the smile on Shannon's face."

"I know. It makes me nervous."

"I'm a bit nervous about this weekend, too. But maybe we should just be happy about her improvement."

"I am." He crossed his arms. "Or I would be, if it all didn't seem so... I don't know..." With no idea how to put his misgivings into words, he could only shrug. He pulled the zippered pouch from his coat pocket. "Before I forget, Dr. Yoshida sent this along. It's Shannon's meds and instructions for the weekend."

"Oh, right. She said you'd be bringing it." Julia took the information page from the packet. Reading silently, she nodded.

Lane peered over her shoulder. "Anything I should know?"

"Only that she needs to be returned to Mercy Cottage no later than six o'clock tomorrow evening. If you'd rather not make the drive again, I'm happy to take her."

"No problem. I'll need to pick up Tate and Rowena anyway."

Disappointment flickered across her expression. "Of course. I forgot." She went back to perusing the instructions, then checked her watch. "Looks like it's almost time for one of Shannon's meds. Would you mind getting her a glass of water?"

He did as she asked.

After Shannon dutifully swallowed her meds, Julia started to the kitchen with the empty glass. Crossing in front of Lane, she smiled. "We'll be fine here if there's anything else you need to be doing."

He'd been debating whether to stick around—Shannon *was* his daughter, after all—or head back to the cabin and catch up on some work. Guess that answered his question.

Julia sensed Lane's dilemma, and she felt bad for him. Maybe she should have invited him to stay awhile, but with Shannon utterly ignoring him, the whole situation felt too strained.

Instead, she made up her mind to provide Shannon with plenty of support and encouragement while subtly inserting enough of the right things into their conversations to soften the girl's heart toward her dad and the home she'd grown up in.

It wasn't long before Shannon's efforts at remaining cheerful began to waver. She lost patience with Tate when he had a minor meltdown over misplacing a toy, and again during lunch when he repeatedly tried to feed part of his tortilla rollup to the dogs. Julia had to intervene by ushering the animals out to the backyard, then took Tate onto her lap and coaxed him to finish his meal. When mother and son retreated to the bedroom for an afternoon nap, Julia felt like she needed one herself. She let the dogs inside and stretched out on the den sofa.

She hadn't realized she'd fallen asleep until a pudgy finger poked her cheek. Blinking, she rolled onto her side. "Hi, Tater Tot." Apparently, the boy had figured out how to escape the portable crib. "Did you have a good nap?"

"Uh-huh. I wake now." Nudging Daisy and Dash from their comfy nest by her feet, he crawled up beside them at the end of the sofa. Moments later, Rowena came over to rest her chin on Tate's knees.

The ring of Julia's cell phone sounded from down the hall. She thought she'd left her phone on the charger in the kitchen. When had she taken it to her room? Easing upright, she shook off her grogginess and reached for Tate's hand. "Better come with Grammy while I find my phone."

Reaching the hallway, she nearly ran into Shannon.

"I, um…" The girl wore a frozen look as if she'd been caught shoplifting. She swallowed and handed Julia the ringing phone. "I wanted to set an alarm so I didn't sleep too long."

"That's fine. Thanks." She read her mother's name on the screen and excused herself to answer. "Hi, Mom. Is everything okay?"

"That's what I was going to ask you. How's the visit going?"

Keeping a smile on her face, she waited while Shannon and Tate continued on to the den. "Mostly good." She lowered her voice to a whisper. "I'm probably overcompensating, but I feel like I need to be hyperalert."

"It was brave of you to take on this responsibility."

"Not really." She peeked into the den, finding Shannon and Tate snuggled in an easy chair and paging through a storybook. "I just hope it helps."

The rest of the afternoon passed without incident, with Shannon seeming more settled as the day went on. Occasionally, a glazed look would come into her eyes, as if melancholy was setting in, but she'd eventually find her smile again and return to playing with her son.

Tate was eating up the attention, too, giggling and doing silly dances and rolling on the floor with the dogs. In another sense, it was as if he was trying every trick he knew to keep his mother's spirits up.

Later, Julia served a simple supper of lemon-pepper chicken with rice pilaf and green beans. After dinner, she helped Shannon give Tate his bath. With the boy clad in footed jammies and smelling like lavender-scented baby wash, Julia left mother and son propped in the guest bed reading a bedtime story while she went to get Shannon's evening meds and a glass of water.

When she returned, both of them had drifted off. The book

lay open atop the coverlet, and Rowena snoozed on her blanket at the foot of the bed. After transferring Tate to the portable crib, she roused Shannon long enough to swallow her meds, then turned out the lights and pulled the door partway closed.

Retreating to the den, she decided Lane would appreciate an update and sent him a text: A few ups and downs but overall a good day. Both are sound asleep now.

Several minutes passed before he responded with a brief Thanks. See you tomorrow afternoon.

Apparently, he was still feeling the sting of rejection, and she couldn't blame him. I hate how she snubbed you this morning, she texted back. We can both stretch our faith muscles and pray for things to go better next time.

He shot her a thumbs-up and the praying hands emoji.

Too bad they couldn't talk in real time and reassure each other, perhaps even pray together.

She laughed to herself. A month ago, she'd never have imagined she'd turn to God in prayer—least of all with a man she was beginning to care for more than she'd ever intended to.

More than she'd ever thought possible.

Those were thoughts best set aside for another time. Yawning, she decided an early bedtime was a good idea after the day she'd had. On her way through the kitchen to let Daisy and Dash have a quick trip outside, she remembered her phone had never finished charging, so she plugged it in.

After making sure the house was secure, she peeked in on Shannon and Tate once more. Leaving her bedroom door ajar so she could hear them if they needed anything, she crawled into bed.

It felt as if she'd barely closed her eyes when Daisy's and Dash's frantic yipping jolted her awake. Sitting up, she fumbled for the switch on the bedside lamp and squinted as her eyes adjusted. Both dogs were racing from the bed to the closed door and back, while Rowena's deep-throated barks came from the other side.

"What in the world…" Grabbing her robe, she yanked open her door and hurried across the hall to the darkened guest room. She flipped the light switch. "Shannon? Are you—"

The room was empty.

"Shannon! Tate!" Choking on her own panicked cry, she spun around and almost tripped over Rowena. When the panting, wide-eyed dog spun around and galloped toward the front door, Julia darted after her.

Gripping Rowena's collar to keep the dog from running out, she pulled open the door. Just then, headlights flashed across the lawn as a car roared away. It took all Julia's strength to keep Rowena from tearing off after it.

Which told her one thing. Tate was in that car, and now he was gone.

Chapter Thirteen

Lane had never driven down the mountain so fast in his life.

Julia's text had come through just past midnight, startling him as he sat in the living room trying to lose himself in a suspense novel. Alone in the cabin for the first night since Shannon had shown up with his surprise grandson, he'd found sleep elusive.

Please, God. Please, God. Please, God. It wasn't much of a prayer, but he was desperate. Desperate to make it to Julia's in one piece, hopefully without leaving any roadkill in his wake. And desperate to learn exactly how a mentally ill young mother and her toddler son could so easily have disappeared into the night.

Screeching to a stop in Julia's driveway, he bolted from the truck. He found her barefoot and coatless on the front porch, shivering as much from worry as from the cold.

"I'm sorry. I'm so sorry," she repeated through half-frozen lips.

Part of him knew he should try to reassure her, but his terrified rage wouldn't let him. He took her by the shoulders and turned her toward the door. "You're chilled to the bone. Let's go inside."

Three anxious dogs blocked their passage. Rowena whined and paced as the dachshunds wove between her long legs.

Once they got past the tangle of canines, Lane demanded to

see the note Julia had found. She fetched it from beneath her cell phone on the kitchen counter and handed it to him with trembling fingers. He skimmed quickly, then read the note again, each word like an ice shard to his heart:

> I know what my dad's trying to do. I'll NEVER let him have my son. This was the only way we could get away. Remember, I told you the first time we met that you were the answer to my prayer? I realize now this chance you've given me is why. Shannon

He drew a pained breath and faced Julia. "You were supposed to be looking after them. How could you let this happen?"

"How was I to know what she was planning?" An indignant spark flashed in her eyes. "Maybe you should be asking yourself where she got the idea that you intended to take Tate away from her permanently."

"But I wouldn't—" He swallowed. Was it possible something he'd said about the guardianship arrangements had given his daughter the wrong impression?

"Lane, I'm sorry. I know you'd never have threatened her with anything like that." A sob caught in Julia's throat. Convulsing, she felt her way to a chair. "You're right, this is my fault. I should have been paying better attention. I should have seen the signs—"

"Stop, stop." Moving behind her, he massaged her shoulders while attempting to corral his racing thoughts. "We're not helping anything by blaming each other or ourselves. Did you call Dr. Yoshida?"

"I was too scared and embarrassed." She shifted to look up at him. "Oh, Lane, this is awful. How can I tell her I let Shannon run away with Tate?"

"First of all, you didn't *let* Shannon run away." He pulled her to her feet and held her trembling body against his chest.

How could he be upset with her when he had years to atone for? "We'll find them, Julia. I'll call the doctor and explain what happened, and then…somehow…we'll find them."

His call roused the doctor from sleep, but once she grasped the situation, she came quickly alert.

"I have you on speaker," he told her, positioning the phone on the table between Julia and himself. "Should we call the police? Go looking for her ourselves?"

"First of all, try not to panic," Dr. Yoshida said.

"Too late for that."

"I understand, but it won't help." The doctor took a deep breath. "Shannon left of her own volition, correct?"

"Yes, but—"

"She is an adult. *And* she voluntarily committed herself for mental health treatment. Those factors alone mean she isn't, legally speaking, a missing person. However, you were granted emergency temporary custody of her son, and that puts her actions in a completely different light."

Julia drew her brows together. "Which means…what?"

Lane's jaw clenched. "It means this could be considered a kidnapping."

"That's true," the doctor said. "So unless you have some idea about where Shannon could have gone, you may want to bring in the police."

"I can't do that to my daughter." Lane firmly shook his head. "Treating her like a criminal would turn her against me forever."

Dr. Yoshida sighed. "I sympathize with your predicament. But you must also think of your grandson and what's best for him—especially considering Shannon's current emotional state."

Julia gripped Lane's hand. "You know Shannon would never intentionally hurt Tate. It's why she brought him home to you in the first place."

Lane lowered his head and groaned. "Then what should we do, Doctor? What *can* we do?"

"You could start by reaching out to any of Shannon's friends or acquaintances, anyone she might have called on to help her with this plan."

He racked his brain. "She left home so long ago that I wouldn't know where to begin."

"Julia?" the doctor said. "Can you think of any of your late son's friends she might still have contact with?"

"I... I can try."

"Good. You work on that, and I will review Shannon's session notes for anything relevant she may have mentioned. Call me if you have any news at all."

"We will," Lane said. "Thank you."

"There's one more thing you can do," Dr. Yoshida added, her tone softening. "Pray."

Lane thanked the doctor again and ended the call. Scooting his chair closer to Julia's, he took her hands. "Pray with me?"

She nodded.

"Dear God," he began, head bowed. His throat closed, and he couldn't continue. From somewhere in his far distant memories of church and Sunday school came fragments of a Bible passage, something about the Spirit interceding when words wouldn't come. He hoped it was true, that God already knew his deepest longings, the unutterable pleas swelling his chest until the only sound he could make was an anguished moan.

Silently, Julia moved onto his lap and wrapped her arms around his neck. As she wept into the folds of his shirt, he pressed her close and gave in to his own tumble of emotions.

Soon, a furry muzzle nosed between them. Rowena whimpered as if to say, *Enough already. Find my boy!*

The interruption was enough to spur him into action. Spying a tissue box, he snatched a handful and pressed them into

Julia's hand while easing her onto her own chair. After grabbing a tissue for himself and blowing his nose, he said, "Are you ready to do some brainstorming?"

"I think so." She glanced around as if getting her bearings. "I never shut down Steven's Facebook account after..." She shuddered. "It's likely at least a few of his friends knew about Shannon."

"Then let's start there."

Julia situated her laptop on the table so she and Lane could both see the screen. It took a megadose of willpower to open Facebook and click on Steven's profile.

When his smiling, bright-eyed image came up, she nearly collapsed.

Lane's strong arms surrounded her, giving her strength. "Hang in there, Julia. You can do this."

After several shaky breaths and a few more tissues, she tried again. Steven's feed contained a seemingly endless string of his friends' posts expressing sorrow over his death and sharing photos and memories. The only way she could push through was to remind herself their goal was to find where Shannon had taken Tate.

"Tell me again when Steven and Shannon got married?"

Lane gave her the date, and she scrolled rapidly backward until she reached posts from that year. The only pictures she found of Shannon also included others in Steven's circle of friends, and in situations that hadn't suggested to Julia that he was in a serious relationship.

"That photo with Shannon and Steven at the lake," Lane said, pointing at the screen. "Do you know the other couple they're with?"

She took a closer look. In hindsight, it became all too clear that when this photo was taken, Steven and Shannon were already much more than friends. Had Julia seen only what she'd wanted to see—a young man following his mother's admonition to keep relationships platonic and focus on his studies?

You don't have time for this. Not with her grandson's well-being at stake.

Swallowing hard, she focused on the image. "That's Eric Davison. He was one of Steven's best friends."

"And the girl?"

Julia scanned the tags. "Claudia Garza. I remember now that she and Eric got engaged not long after this picture was taken."

After which, she'd cautioned Steven again about avoiding romantic entanglements and keeping his eye on the goal. *Her* goal, she admitted with a pinch to her heart.

She clicked over to Eric's Facebook profile. Since she wasn't in his friends list, she couldn't dig any deeper, but his cover photo of a wedding party in front of a church indicated he and Claudia had gotten married.

"Wait, that's Shannon." Lane leaned closer. "See? The last girl on the right. She's one of the bridesmaids."

Julia recognized her now. She was reed-thin and looked as if she'd had to dredge her smile from the depths of her being, and for only as long as it would take to snap the photo. "This had to be after Steven…" Her throat clenched. "After Tate was born."

Lane gently squeezed her shoulder. "If Shannon was in the wedding party, she and Claudia must have been close. They could still be in touch. Do you know how to reach Claudia? Or her husband?"

"I only knew them through Steven, and not well at all." She vaguely remembered accepting Eric's condolences at the funeral. "I don't even recall where Eric is from."

Lane's frustrated sigh whispered past her ear. "Can you

maybe post a message or something? I have no idea how Face-book works."

Sinking into the chair, she rubbed her temples. "I can, but since I'm not on Eric's or Claudia's friends list, they may not see the message for days or weeks or…ever."

He shoved to his feet and stalked to the counter. "I can't think anymore without coffee."

"I'll make some." She went to the cupboard for the canister. "What time is it, anyway?"

"A little past five."

Had they been at this that long already? No wonder her eyes felt like sandpaper.

Lane filled the reservoir while she measured coffee grounds. "We should eat something, too," he said. "I can scramble some eggs."

"I couldn't." Her stomach heaved at the mere suggestion of food. That meant full-strength java wasn't going to sit very well, but she'd done it before when in crunch mode.

The dogs, who'd settled down a bit as the night wore on, now paced at the kitchen door. Julia released them into the yard and then scooped kibble into their bowls. They weren't likely to complain about an early breakfast.

Daisy and Dash didn't, anyway. After Julia let the dogs back inside, Rowena turned up her nose at the bowl and lay staring at the front door as if Tate were sure to return through it any moment now.

The dog's sullen posture only increased Julia's burden of guilt. She'd convinced Lane that having Shannon stay with her would work out for the best. Could she have been more wrong?

"Julia." Lane touched her arm. "Coffee's ready. I'm making myself some toast. Sure you don't want some?"

She waved away the offer and filled two mugs while Lane buttered his toast. Returning to the computer, she composed messages to both Eric and Claudia that she hoped wouldn't come across as too alarming or desperate. *Please contact me if you hear from Shannon*, she concluded. *I only want to help.*

"It's done," she said, closing her laptop.

"So now we wait." Legs extended under the table, Lane nursed his coffee and gazed into the distance. After only one or two bites, his toast remained untouched.

Real or imagined, she felt his judgment. "If I could think of anyone else to reach out to, don't you think I would? After Steven died, it would have cost me too much emotional pain to try to stay in touch with any of his friends. I never even opened most of the sympathy cards. I just stuffed them in the bottom drawer of my desk."

Casting a glance her way, he gave a humorless laugh. "About three years after Tessa's funeral, I came across the shoebox where I'd stashed the cards I'd received. I tossed the whole box into the recycle bin without opening a single one."

"Oh, Lane, that's so sad. Now you'll never know what people who knew and loved your wife wanted to share with you."

He lifted one shoulder in a weak sign of agreement. "All I cared about then was forgetting the past and starting over." Sliding his hand over hers, he asked, "Are *you* at the point where you could bear to read those cards and letters? Will you ever be?"

"Maybe not yet," she replied softly, "but I want to be. Because that's when I'll know I'm finally coming out on the other side of my grief."

The other side of grief. Lane wondered if he could pinpoint exactly when thoughts of Tessa hadn't made him want to double over from the pain ripping through his gut. Having a growing daughter to focus on had helped, and he still believed he'd done the right thing by ditching his former life and career and starting from scratch in the mountains.

Well…mostly. He never should have taken it to such isolating extremes. All through Shannon's childhood, the Vernons had tried to tell him she needed so much more than a lonely, sheltered life on the mountain. Why hadn't he listened?

After two more mugs of coffee, he was ready to climb out of his skin. Tired as he was—he hadn't slept since dawn yesterday—he couldn't allow himself to sit still long enough to grab a quick nap. Not while his daughter and grandson were missing.

Over the past hour or so, Julia had posted messages to three or four other friends of Steven's who might also know Shannon. Returning to the table, he asked, "Did you check for replies again?"

"I just did ten minutes ago." Elbows resting on either side of her laptop, she rubbed her eyes. "It's only a little past seven on a Sunday morning. Sensible people are still sound asleep."

"Can you think of anyone else you could contact? Judging from Steven's Facebook page, he didn't lack for friends." He immediately regretted his impatient tone. Drawing a chair closer to hers, he shifted her to face him. "I didn't mean to snap. But I feel like I'm going to lose it if we don't get answers soon."

"I know. Me, too." She lifted red-rimmed eyes to his before turning back to her computer. "I'll look through Steven's timeline again. Maybe more names will jump out at me."

"No. Stop. You've done all you can for now. You're exhausted." He pulled her to her feet and propelled her to the den sofa with an arm around her waist. "Close your eyes. Try to get some rest."

"Only if you do the same."

Pulling out his phone, he nodded and sank into the easy chair. "Okay, one hour. I'm setting my alarm."

And so the day went. He and Julia took turns catnapping between checking her laptop for replies. When they'd heard nothing by late afternoon, he had no choice but to head home and take care of his livestock. He couldn't expect the Vernons to cover for him indefinitely.

He hated to leave Julia, though. Her haggard look worried him, and he was at a loss for anything more he could say or do to convince her she wasn't to blame.

"At least let me call Maddie and Witt," he said, smoothing her tangled hair off her face. "Besides, they're probably wondering why we didn't make it to church this morning."

He'd hardly spoken the words when Julia's cell phone rang. She spun away to grab it. Shoulders collapsing as she read the caller's name, she cast Lane a weary smile. "It's Maddie. She must have read your mind."

He supported her with an arm around her waist as she tearfully described what had happened. When the call ended, she pivoted and sank against Lane's chest. "Maddie and Witt are coming over," she said. "I couldn't talk them out of it."

"I'm glad." He kissed the top of her head. "You shouldn't be alone."

"I wish I could go to the cabin with you."

"Me, too. But you know how bad cell and internet service is up there." Stepping back, he hooked his index finger under her chin and searched her face. "Hey, convince me the tough, tenacious Julia Frasier I know and love is still in there."

She gave a trembling nod. "I'll try."

He stayed with her until the Wittenbauers arrived, and he promised he'd return first thing in the morning—or sooner, if word came. Making his way up the winding mountain roads, he prayed as he never had before. For Shannon. For Tate. And for the woman he'd come to care for at a depth he'd never expected to feel again.

* * *

Maddie's first question after Lane had left was, "What have you eaten today?"

"Not much," Julia admitted. "I haven't felt like I could keep anything down."

"That won't do. Mind if I snoop in your pantry?"

Hunched over the computer again, she gave a dismissive flick of her fingers. She already missed Lane's comforting embrace, his confidence, his strength.

She missed everything about him.

The tough, tenacious Julia Frasier I know and love...

She wasn't feeling particularly tough or tenacious at the moment. And had he meant to use the word *love*...or had it merely been an offhand remark? Because over the course of the past few weeks, her feelings toward him had been inching toward the *L* word.

Inching? How about moving at the speed of light?

But would he ever forgive her—ever truly be able to love her—if they never found Shannon and Tate?

Witt pulled over a chair and wrapped her icy fingers in his. "In the Book of Luke, Jesus says, 'For the Son of man is come to seek and to save that which was lost.' It's a truth I can vouch for firsthand. So believe me when I say that wherever Shannon and her little boy are right now, God is watching over them."

All she could do was nod.

While Witt sat praying with her, a savory aroma wafted from the stove. Shortly, Maddie brought a steaming bowl of chicken noodle soup to the table. Nudging Julia's laptop aside, she set the bowl in front of her along with a napkin and spoon. "This should go down easy. And after you've eaten, you're going to bed. Witt and I will monitor your computer and phone for any messages."

"But I—"

"That was a direct order, not a suggestion." Maddie had used her schoolteacher tone, but her smile conveyed tender concern.

It took only one spoonful of soup for Julia to realize how hungry she was. She ate slowly, giving the warm, flavorful broth ample time to settle in her stomach. Afterward, fatigue overwhelming her, she gave in to Maddie's directive and retreated to her bedroom. She fell into a sound sleep the moment her head hit the pillow and didn't know another thing until a shaft of sun pierced her eyelids.

Morning already? She jolted upright. Still wearing yesterday's yoga pants and sweatshirt, she hurried to the kitchen. Witt was just letting the dogs in from the backyard, and Maddie was stirring something on the stove. When they looked her way, she didn't have to ask the question hovering on her lips. Their apologetic smiles told her there'd been no news.

Realizing they'd been here all night, she immediately grew concerned about their sanctuary dogs.

"They're being looked after," Maddie assured. "Two of my best volunteers stepped in." She added a dash of pepper to the pan. "By the way, your mother called a few minutes ago. I gathered she doesn't know what's happened, so I didn't tell her. I just said we came over because you were feeling a little under the weather."

"Thanks. Mom doesn't need anything else to worry about." Julia sank into a chair and began scrolling through email and messages.

It dawned on her that it was Monday, and she should be on her way to the clinic. But how could she possibly concentrate on work?

Because that's what you do. What she'd always done. Becoming adept at compartmentalizing her life was how she'd managed to survive divorce, single parenthood, the loss of her son, her father's illness...

It was how she'd survive this crisis, too.

She closed her laptop. Maddie or Witt had started coffee, so she went to the cupboard for her favorite travel mug. "I'll be taking this to go, just as soon as I clean up and change."

"Change for what?" Maddie demanded.

"Work, of course." Snapping on the lid, she started from the kitchen.

Maddie sucked in a breath. "Are you serious?"

Continuing on, she said over her shoulder, "I can check for messages at my office as easily as I can here. And besides, at least at the clinic I'll feel like I'm accomplishing something."

Chapter Fourteen

Lane had risen before dawn to tend the livestock and deal with the usual morning chores. He'd wanted to text Julia first thing but put it off in hopes that with Witt and Maddie there, she'd been able to get some sleep.

When she replied to his 8:14 a.m. message by saying she was on her way to the clinic, he was more than a little surprised.

Left Rowena with D&D at my house, she texted. I sent M&W home to take care of their own animals. Obviously no news or I would have let you know right away.

Obviously.

He'd prayed for Julia to find her inner strength, but was she striving *too* hard to regain some control?

Once he'd taken care of things at home, he drove to the clinic. Dylan greeted him at the front desk and said Julia had just gone into surgery—routine, he stated, so it shouldn't take long. Lane made himself a coffee and claimed one of the doughnuts someone had brought. He grabbed a fishing magazine from the coffee table and went to Julia's office to wait.

He'd read the magazine from cover to cover twice by the time she strode in forty-five minutes later.

She went straight into his arms. "I was so happy when they told me you were here."

"How are you holding up?" He inhaled the fruity scent of

her freshly washed hair. "You could have taken the day off, you know."

"This is where I needed to be." Heaving a tired sigh, she nestled closer. "Where I'm needed."

I need you, too, he wanted to say. "Promise me you won't overdo it. This could turn into a marathon, not a sprint."

"Which is another reason I have to keep working." She left his arms and moved behind her desk. "While I'm between patients, I should check for messages."

Lane pulled a chair around to join her. When she found no replies from any of Steven's friends, he said, "We should call Dr. Yoshida. Even if she hasn't come up with any new leads, I'd like her input on where we go from here."

What the doctor had to say wasn't reassuring. She left them with the same choices: wait it out while hoping and praying, or take legal action and risk further alienating Shannon...or worse.

It was the *or worse* that held Lane back. He firmly believed his daughter would never endanger her son. But would she fall so far into that deep, dark hole that she'd harm herself? He'd rather never see her or his grandson again than push her toward an act of desperation she could never return from.

"So," he said, "I guess we wait."

Eyes filled with understanding, Julia laced her fingers through his. "I guess we wait."

She was about to return to work when her desk intercom buzzed. Dylan's voice came over the speaker: "Dr. J, you have a call on line two from someone named Eric."

With an anxious glance at Lane, she grabbed the receiver. "Eric? Hello!"

"Hi, Dr. Frasier. Claudia was looking at Facebook this morning and saw your message. She told me I should call you right away. Is everything okay?"

"No, Eric, it isn't. May I put you on speaker? I'm with someone who needs to hear our conversation." At his assent, she introduced Lane and told Eric in as few words as possible why she'd reached out. "We're hoping one of Steven's friends might know where Shannon could have gone."

Eric remained silent for several seconds. "Sorry, but no. We haven't heard from her. Honestly, until just now, I wasn't sure if you'd ever found out Steven got married. He wanted to tell you, right up until the end, but..."

"Then why—" Julia's voice broke. She closed her eyes and swallowed hard. "Why didn't he?"

Heart aching for her, Lane took her hand and gave it an encouraging squeeze.

Eric cleared his throat. "I'm not sure I should say anything, but since Steven can't anymore..."

"Please, just tell me." Julia gave a hard sniff. "Not knowing is destroying me."

Haltingly, Eric admitted what Steven had confided in him nearly four years ago. He'd begun to feel pressure about joining the family veterinary practice, and he'd concluded it wasn't the right path for him.

"He never wanted to let you down, and he struggled a long time with how and when to break the news to you." He paused and inhaled deeply. "This may be more than you want to hear, Dr. Frasier, but the day of his accident, he was on his way home to tell you everything."

Silent tears slid down her face. Lane swiveled her chair toward him and pulled her into his arms. Speaking toward the phone, he said roughly, "Thank you, Eric. If Shannon does happen to contact you, please let us know."

"I will, sir. Wish I could have been more helpful."

Lane pressed the disconnect button. He cradled Julia on his lap and smoothed back her hair while she sobbed.

Face buried in his shoulder, she murmured through her tears, "How could my son imagine I'd ever be disappointed in him? I thought he *wanted* to become a vet. If I'd only known sooner—"

"Hush, don't do this to yourself." He made her sit up and look at him. "You think I haven't asked myself a million times how I could have been a better father for Shannon? But we're only human. No matter how hard we try to do the right thing, we'll still make mistakes."

"I know, but—"

"But nothing." Truth dawning, he gave in to a crooked smile. "I think I'm finally getting what Witt and Pastor Peters tried to tell me the first time I met with them. God knows we're helpless, self-centered, mistake-prone human beings, but He loves us anyway. It's the whole reason He sent us Jesus, so we can quit wallowing in our guilt and start living—*really* living."

Julia slid back into her own chair and pulled a handful of tissues from a desk drawer. Dabbing her eyes, she said, "You make it sound too easy."

"I thought the same thing at first. But reading the Bible again has reminded me that God's ways are so much higher than ours. I think He *wants* to make it easy for us to come to Him." He lifted his hand to her cheek and thumbed away a teardrop she'd missed. "He just asks us to believe. The rest will follow."

Long after Lane had gone, his words played through Julia's mind. Just as with every other area of her life, had she been attempting to manage her interaction with God instead of simply letting Him in? She imagined God's amusement over the disconnect between her intentions and her follow-through. What good were promises to trust Him if she continually resorted to doing things her own way?

She recalled years ago hearing an inspirational speaker pose the question, "Are you a human *being*, or a human *doing*?"

At the time, she'd smothered an annoyed chuckle, because what did sitting around and waiting accomplish? Her ex-husband's irresponsibility had ingrained in her the value—no, the *necessity*—of direct action, because if she didn't do something, whether taking care of the house or raising their son or bringing home a regular paycheck, it didn't get done.

But the events of last weekend were driving home a truth she continually tried to sidestep.

You are not in control, Julia, and you never were.

Leaving an exam room, she offered a brief smile to Dr. Ramirez as she strode her way. The young veterinarian was already proving her worth, as was Dr. Kruger. In fact, the clients had taken well to all three new staff members. Julia paused and dipped her chin in silent gratitude. God had sent her two skilled vets and a competent office manager exactly when she needed them.

"Dr. Frasier?" Nikki Ramirez lightly touched her arm. "Are you okay?"

"Yes—actually, no." She suddenly found herself unwilling to pretend otherwise. "I—I'm dealing with some personal issues." Gaze softening, she tilted her head. "And I know I've said you can call me Julia."

"Sorry, it's hard when I have so much respect for you... *Julia*." Nikki gave a self-conscious laugh before growing serious. "If you need to take care of something, Dr. Kruger and I can cover the rest of today's appointments."

"Thanks, but things are in kind of a holding pattern. There's nothing to be done right now."

"Except possibly to take a little time for yourself? You've been going almost nonstop since your visitor left this morning."

At the mention of Lane, her heart flipped. She'd like nothing better than to head straight to the cabin and into his arms.

But no, she needed to stay in town where she could be reached if any of the contacts she'd made responded with news.

She flicked a loose strand of hair off her forehead. "I appreciate your concern, Nikki, but staying busy keeps my mind off the things I have no control over." With a rueful smile, she added, "Which I'm learning is pretty much everything."

A midafternoon coffee break kept her going long enough to finish the day. Before leaving that morning, Lane had asked if he could pick up Rowena and take her back to the cabin with him, so she came home to just Daisy and Dash, who happily cuddled in her lap for a few minutes. She zapped a frozen meal for herself, and after the dogs had their supper, they trotted between the front and back doors as if missing their giant-size playmate as much as she missed Lane.

Deciding it was time to let her parents know what was going on, she called her mother. Mom was stunned but supportive, saying she could get a neighbor to sit with Dad for a day or two if Julia needed her at the clinic. She assured her mother she was coping for now but wouldn't hesitate to ask for help if things changed.

Next, she called Maddie, only to say there'd been no news as of yet. As they said goodbye, a text came through from Lane, and they spent the next half hour texting back and forth about how their days had gone and generally attempting to keep each other's spirits up. Lane signed off with a texted prayer that brought a lump to Julia's throat.

Getting ready for bed later, she wondered if she'd ever have rediscovered her faith if not for everything that had happened since Lane had come into her life. As frightening and difficult as the past few days had been, she didn't know how she'd get through this ordeal without Lane's support combined with the love and provision of a sovereign God.

Tuesday passed much the same. Then Wednesday and Thursday, still with no word from Shannon or anyone she may have reached out to. Julia made it through each day only by the power of prayer and the faith that wherever Shannon and Tate had disappeared to, God watched over them.

Early Friday morning, while she stood shivering on the patio and waited for Daisy and Dash to take care of business, her cell phone chimed in the pocket of her velour robe. She'd been carrying it with her at all times, but after so many days with no news, she assumed it was her mother's regular call.

Herding the dogs inside, she answered without looking at the display. "Good morning, Mom."

"J-Julia?" The stammering, panicked voice was definitely not her mother's. "Please, y-you've got to help me!"

Her stomach clenched. Kicking the door shut, she pressed the phone hard against her ear. "Shannon. Where are you?"

"I—I can't—" The girl sounded like she was hyperventilating. Tate's incessant crying sounded in the background.

"What's wrong with Tate?" Julia demanded. "Is he sick? Is he hurt?"

"No, but he won't stop crying, and I—" Shannon's voice rose with every word until she was practically screaming. "He just wants his dog, and he won't shut up about it!"

Julia inhaled slowly, deeply. *Please, Lord, give me the words.* "Shannon, honey, I need you to try to calm down and listen, okay? Because your anxiety isn't helping Tate." She tried for a light laugh. "I remember when Steven used to obsess over something, and if I let him upset me, too, it was a lot harder to quiet him."

"Okay…okay…" Shannon expelled a tremulous gust of

air, while nearby, Tate's sobs grew louder. "But could we just come get the dog? Because I can't take this crying anymore. I just can't!"

It didn't take a mental health pro to realize the girl was spiraling. Maybe Julia could use this to her advantage. "If you tell me where you are, I could—"

"No. I'd rather come there. My friend can watch Tate till I get back."

So that strategy wasn't going to work. "The thing is, Rowena isn't at my house anymore. Your dad took her home to the cabin."

Shannon grew silent except for her strained breathing.

Tate's howls continued. "Want Weena! "P'ease, Mama, now!"

Julia's heart broke over the little boy's despairing cries. She had to think of something. "Shannon, listen. I know how you feel about seeing your dad again, but if you want to get the dog, I'm afraid you'll have to go to the cabin. I can meet you there, though. You'd hardly have to see your dad at all, just get Rowena and leave."

A sniffle. "Really?"

"Yes, really. I'd just ask one thing of you, though."

"Wh-what's that?"

She sent up a silent prayer that her request wouldn't slam the door on this discussion. "Bring Tate with you so your dad can tell him a final goodbye. Please. You can spare him that much compassion."

Shannon's silence stretched thin, until she finally murmured, "I... I guess so."

Eyes squeezed shut, Julia pressed a hand to her racing heart. "Thank you." She lowered the phone long enough to make sure it showed the number Shannon had called from. "Can I text you back at this same number when I've arranged a time to meet?"

"Yes, okay. Soon, though." Speaking away from the phone, she said, "It'll be all right, sweetie. Mama's going to get your doggy for you."

A little boy's hiccuping cry was the last thing Julia heard before the line went dead.

She immediately sent a text to Lane: Heard from Shannon! Working on a plan. Can you come over?

His reply came seconds later: See you in an hour.

A quick call to the clinic caught Amy tending to preopening duties. "Something's come up, and I can't make it in today. If things get too backed up, my mom has offered to be on call."

"Don't worry about a thing, Dr. J. We've got your back."

She thanked the Lord again for the caring and dependable staff He'd given her.

After feeding the dogs and starting coffee, she phoned her mother to fill her in and asked her to please pray the plan worked.

After nearly a week of waiting and wondering, could they be close to getting Tate and Shannon back? *Please, Lord*, Lane prayed as he rushed through his morning chores, *whatever Julia has in mind, let it work*.

Shortly after eight thirty, he parked in her driveway. She met him at the door with the hug he'd been craving and then ushered him to the kitchen. Dressed in jeans, a turtleneck and a fleece vest, she looked more beautiful—and more hopeful—than he'd seen her in days.

"Don't keep me in suspense," he said as he accepted a mug of strong coffee. "What did Shannon say? And what's this plan you're working on?"

She gave him the gist of Shannon's phone call. His chest squeezed as he pictured his distraught grandson.

"The first thing we need to do," she said, "is talk to Dr.

Yoshida. She should be there when Shannon brings Tate to the cabin."

"I see where you're going with this." He tweaked his chin. "Like an intervention?"

"Exactly. We need to lovingly convince her that running away isn't the solution. That she must go back into treatment. She may not trust either of us right now, but I believe she trusts her doctor enough to listen."

Dr. Yoshida agreed the plan had merit. They talked through the timing and decided to ask Shannon to come that afternoon at three o'clock. Dr. Yoshida would arrive an hour earlier so they could discuss any last-minute details.

After Julia called her parents with another update, Lane followed her to their house to drop off Daisy and Dash in case this turned into a longer day than anticipated.

At the cabin, Lane parked in his usual spot under the deck, and Julia pulled in behind him. Her lime-green SUV would be in plain sight to assure Shannon that she'd kept her promise to be there. He'd have Dr. Yoshida park out of sight.

Over a lunch of Lane's homemade vegetable soup neither of them had much appetite for, they reviewed every possibility—good, bad or downright horrible—as to how the afternoon could go. The initial excitement quickly wore thin, replaced by nerves and doubt. For Julia's sake, Lane fought to stay positive, but all he could think about was what he'd do if they didn't convince his daughter to leave Tate with him and return to the hospital.

Dr. Yoshida arrived a few minutes after two. While Julia showed her inside, Lane took her keys and moved her car to the other side of the barn.

The doctor's serenely confident demeanor allayed some of their anxiety. She reminded them to remain calm no matter how Shannon reacted, and above all, to trust the Holy Spirit for the words to speak.

As it neared three o'clock, Lane's pulse ramped up. According to plan, he took Rowena upstairs and shut her in the bedroom. She wasn't happy about it, but it was one more stalling tactic to keep Shannon from bolting.

Back downstairs, he distracted himself with a sudoku puzzle while Julia watched from the living room window. At five after three, she called him over as a blue sedan slowly approached the open gate and turned in. A woman he didn't recognize was driving. Shannon sat in the passenger seat.

He turned toward Dr. Yoshida. "She's here."

Julia hauled in a deep breath and started for the door. "That's my cue."

"Wait." Lane cut her off and wrapped her in his arms. "I'll be praying. For all of us."

"I'm counting on it." Casting him a shaky smile, she reluctantly slipped from his embrace and stepped out to the deck.

Lane returned to the window he'd left open slightly so he could hear what was said. Dr. Yoshida joined him, both of them staying out of view while peering around the curtain.

The blue car eased to a stop next to Julia's SUV, and now Lane could make out the top of Tate's head in a child's seat in the back. He dipped his chin in a sigh of relief. His greatest worry was that his daughter would decide not to bring Tate after all, and if this intervention didn't work, how would they ever find him?

After a moment's hesitation, Shannon opened the passenger door, her gaze nervously skimming the area as she stood beside the car. "Where's the dog?"

"In the cabin," Julia replied calmly. "It's okay. I've talked with your dad, and he understands what you want. We'd both be so grateful if we could spend a little time with Tate before you go."

Arms crossed, Shannon glanced over her shoulder. "Well…

just for a few minutes. I don't want to be here any longer than I have to."

"Of course." Julia edged closer, all smiles. "Can I help you get him out of the car?"

"No, I'll do it." Leaning into the rear seat to unbuckle Tate, Shannon said something to the driver, who nodded.

When she emerged with the little boy, his lips were trembling and his face was blotchy from crying. Lane would have charged out the door to grab him if Dr. Yoshida hadn't held him in place with her amazingly strong grip.

"Remember what we talked about," she reminded him. "Whatever you're feeling right now, don't let Shannon see anything but her loving, concerned father." She gave his arm a final pat and slipped out to the kitchen, where she'd stay until Shannon and Tate were settled in the living room.

When Julia and Shannon started up the outer stairs, Lane swallowed his mounting anxiety and crossed to the other side of the room. He'd give his daughter plenty of space so she wouldn't feel cornered.

The door opened. Julia entered first, casting Lane a subtle nod. As they'd agreed, once Shannon and Tate passed through the door, Julia closed it and reached up to silently secure the safety latch. It wouldn't keep Shannon from bolting if she decided to, but it might slow her getaway.

"Me down!" Tate demanded. He wriggled in Shannon's arms until she had no choice but to release him. He ran to Rowena's empty bed near the woodstove and swung his gaze in all directions. "Weena? Weena!"

"It's okay, Tater Tot." Lane knelt and held out his arms to the whimpering boy. Judging from the muted scratching and whining coming from upstairs, Rowena sensed her best pal was near, but she'd have to wait a little longer. "I'll get her for you in a few minutes. We just need to talk to Mama first."

"I'm not here to talk." Rushing over, Shannon grabbed Tate's hand before Lane could scoop him up. She raised her glance toward the noises and then turned to Julia. Her voice shook as she stated, "Y-you promised we could get the dog and leave."

"Yes, and you also promised we could have a little time with our grandson. Please. Just five minutes." The smile never left Julia's face.

Lane didn't know how she managed, because he was about to lose it big-time. Pushing to his feet, he prayed for a measure of Julia's self-control. "How about we all sit down? Hey, I have some of that cocoa mix you always liked. Can I fix you a cup?"

Breath coming in quick gasps, Shannon appeared on the edge of a full-blown breakdown. "I—I just want—"

Dr. Yoshida quietly entered the room. "Hello, Shannon."

Her chin dropped. "Wh-what are you doing here?"

"I thought you might need a friendly face." The doctor moved closer, one hand extended. "Will you let me help?"

"Mama?" Tate tugged on his mother's hand, his little face turned up and his lower lip pushed out in a pleading look. "It be otay."

That broke her completely. Sobbing, she collapsed into the rocking chair and pulled her son into her lap. Dr. Yoshida knelt in front of her, speaking so softly that Lane couldn't hear. Shannon nodded, her expression compliant, and that had to be a good sign.

Thank You, Lord!

Chapter Fifteen

A full two weeks had gone by since Shannon had returned to Mercy Cottage—voluntarily, for which Julia gave thanks every single day. Back on the meds Shannon had neglected to take while in hiding, the young mom was slowly stabilizing. In the meantime, Tate was safe and secure at the cabin with his grandpa and his faithful dog.

That was all well and good—wonderful, in fact—but it left Julia with one significant problem. With things returning to a semblance of normal, including her work at the clinic, weekends were her only real chance to see her grandson.

And Lane. She couldn't forget Lane.

Too distracted by everything that had happened recently, they'd both been avoiding a closer examination of their relationship. Julia's heart was telling her she wanted it to be more...but did Lane still feel the same? Or, now that his focus had returned to taking care of Tate and monitoring Shannon's improvement, would it be easier all around if they scaled things back to the friendship level?

She hoped to get a sense of his feelings soon—possibly even today.

Leaving Drs. Ramirez and Kruger to cover the Saturday morning clinic appointments, Julia aimed her SUV up the winding mountain road to Lane's cabin. The first weekend in November had turned decidedly colder, but the sky remained a clear wintry blue. The comforting scent of woodsmoke seeped through the air vents as she passed other homesteads on the way up. She pictured Lane's cozy living room, the red-orange glow of his stove, Rowena stretched out on her bed nearby and Tate stacking blocks on the nubby carpet.

She imagined walking into Lane's arms and inhaling his manly scents of piney aftershave and flannel.

She imagined his kiss...

Jerking her attention back to the road, she gave herself a mental talking-to. No point in getting her hopes up in case recent events had permanently cooled things between them. Lane may have forgiven her for her part in Shannon's disappearance, and he'd shown nothing but kindness and reassurance ever since. But shared hugs and chaste kisses didn't tell the whole story. A man who'd chosen to hide away from the world for twenty-plus years after the death of his wife could just as easily decide that giving his heart again wasn't worth the risk.

It was half past nine when she braked outside his ranch gate. Stepping from her car to open the gate, she inhaled a bracing breath of clean mountain air. Something cold and wet brushed her cheek, and she looked skyward to see a few tiny snowflakes swirling in the breeze. The clouds creeping in didn't appear too heavy, but this was Montana in the mountains, and the weather could change quickly.

Not *too* quickly today—*please, Lord*—because she was counting on a full day's visit with her grandson.

And with Lane.

"Julia." His husky voice startled her. "I didn't expect you until this afternoon."

She looked up to see him striding down the driveway, Tate propped on his hip. Rowena trotted beside them, still favoring her cast rear leg.

Pushing open the gate, Julia tried for a casual smile. "I had a chance to get on the road early. If you have other stuff to do, I can keep Tate entertained and out of your way."

Mouth in a twist, he glanced toward his workshop. "I do need to finish a project I've been working on."

"Perfect." She came just close enough to plant a kiss on Tate's cheek and then took a giant step back. Keeping her smile bright, she said, "Let me get parked at the cabin, and I can take over with the little guy."

After she drove forward, Lane closed the gate and met her at the cabin steps. He had an edginess in his posture that she hadn't noticed the past couple of weekends when she'd either driven up to spend a couple of hours with Tate or they'd met at church on Sunday mornings.

She cocked her head. "If I've come at an inconvenient time—"

"It isn't that. I, uh..."

"Gampy." Tate pinched Lane's chin between his pudgy thumb and fingers, forcing him to make eye contact. The boy's expression was as insistent as Julia had ever seen it. "No wait. Show Gammy."

She narrowed her eyes. "Show me what, Tater Tot?"

"In there." He pointed to the workshop. "Gampy make su'pwise."

"A surprise? For Grammy?" She cast Lane a questioning glance as her heart gave a stutter.

"It isn't ready yet. I was hoping to finish it before you got here." Annoyance filled his tone. His puckered frown reminded her of Tate's when he didn't get his way.

"Well...like I said, Tate and I can go inside and play by ourselves while you...do whatever it is you need to do."

"No, Gampy. Show now!" Tate wriggled so much that Lane had to set him on the ground. He grabbed Lane's fingers and tugged him in the direction of the workshop.

Planting his feet, Lane struggled to keep his balance. "Tate—"

"Now, Gampy!" The boy grunted and pulled harder on Lane's hand. Rowena barked and pranced, her own excitement bubbling over.

He hung his head in defeat. "Okay, okay. But this isn't how I wanted today to go."

Julia almost felt bad for him, but she was too interested to see what her surprise was to let him off the hook. Besides, if he'd gone to all this trouble, it had to mean something about his feelings for her...didn't it?

Nope, this was not at all the way Lane had pictured today going. Julia *never* managed to break away from the clinic on Saturdays early enough to spend the whole day with him and Tate. He'd assumed he'd have at least four or five more hours to put the finishing touches on his project. Then he'd planned to spruce up the cabin before running over to Lila's to pick up the rhubarb pie she was making for tonight's dessert. Lila had even volunteered to keep Tate at her house during dinner so Lane and Julia could have a bit of privacy.

And all this to—he hoped—convince Julia exactly how much she meant to him. Since Shannon had returned to the hospital, they'd been idling in neutral, as if Julia felt as insecure as he did about looking deeper at where they went from here.

"Gampy. C'mon." Tate's tug on his fingers hadn't let up.

"I'm coming, kiddo." Wincing, he motioned for Julia to follow. "I'd intended to save this for later, but I guess we're doing it now."

She caught up and grabbed Tate's other hand. "You made something for me in your workshop?"

His anticipation rose as he imagined her reaction. "Like I

said, it's not all the way done yet." He still needed to apply the last coat of varnish. By late afternoon, it would have been dry enough for the unveiling.

When they were still several steps away, Tate trotted ahead and then stood with his back to the workshop door and stretched out his arms. "Gammy, close eyes."

"Okay." She cast Lane an uncertain glance. "But someone will have to take my hand and guide me."

"Happy to do the honors. Wait right here while I get the door." He couldn't believe how his heart had begun to pound. Would she like it? Or would she see it as either too sentimental or too presumptuous? Or both?

He eased open the door, releasing aromas of sawdust, oil, wood stain and varnish.

Tate bounced on his toes and clapped his hands. "Otay, Gammy. Come see!"

Lane returned to link her arm through his. "Keep your eyes closed. I'll tell you when to look."

Her breaths became quick and shallow as he led her inside.

When he'd positioned her directly in front of his creation, he stepped aside. "You can open your eyes now."

She blinked a few times, gasped and pressed both hands to her heart. "Oh, Lane, how beautiful!"

"Don't touch it yet. I still need to apply another coat." Watching her expression as she examined every inch of the high-backed oak rocking chair, he warmed with pride.

"Lane, is that…" She extended her hand toward the designs he'd carved into the scrolled upper back. "It is! It's the rose of Sharon like my great-grandmother's ring."

"Since you were kind enough to let Shannon keep it, I thought you might like a remembrance."

"It's… It's perfect." A tear slipped down her cheek, and she blotted it with the back of her glove.

Tate sidled up beside her leg and tugged on her jacket. "Gammy like?"

"I sure do, honey. So very much." She scooped him into her arms. "And look there between the roses. That spells 'Grammy.'"

"Gammy!" He clapped his hands. Rowena barked and wagged her tail.

After giving Julia a few more minutes to admire the chair from various angles, Lane suggested she take Tate to the cabin while he applied more varnish. "It won't be ready to take home until it's completely dry, but I could bring it over in a few days."

She pulled her lips between her teeth, her gaze turning thoughtful. "Maybe. We'll see…"

Her remark punctured his enthusiasm. "Hey, I get it. I should have matched it better to your decor—"

"No, I wouldn't change a thing. It's just—" Drawing a quick breath, she brightened her smile. "We can talk about it later. Tater Tot, let's take Rowena to the house. We can play or read a story while we wait for Gramps."

He watched for a moment as they plodded across the yard. Then he latched the door to keep from losing any more warmth from his shop heater.

Great. Now he was left to ponder where he'd gone wrong. Because how did gushing, teary-eyed appreciation do a complete U-turn toward *We'll see* in a matter of seconds?

An hour later, he put away his tools and supplies, slipped into his jacket and closed up the shop. Outside, the clouds had thickened, and the wind had picked up. Before he reached the cabin steps, his coat sleeves looked like they'd been sprinkled with powdered sugar.

So much for his dinner plans. Julia would likely decide to cut her visit short before the weather got any worse.

Inside, he found all three of them—Julia, Tate and Rowena—camped out near the stove on the giant-size fleece-covered dog bed.

Julia looked up from the storybook she'd been reading to Tate. "I helped myself to the rest of your coffee, so I started a fresh pot. It should be ready."

"Thanks. I could use some warming up." It was a convenient excuse to put off a discussion he wasn't sure how to begin. Trying not to think about how beautiful she looked in the red-gold glow of the firelight, he started for the kitchen. "By the way, the snow's picking up. You might want to head home before it gets too heavy."

"Yes, I noticed," she said, startling him. He hadn't realized she'd gotten up to follow. "But your guest room's still available, isn't it?"

His stomach somersaulted. He swallowed hard before swiveling to face her. "It is. But are you sure—"

"I'm sure I'm not ready to leave so soon."

Her tentative smile made his mouth go dry. He returned his attention to what he'd come to the kitchen for, but in his current emotional state, he feared he'd either drop his mug or spill coffee all over the counter and himself.

"Here, let me." She nudged him out of the way and reached for the carafe. "Tate's going to be hungry for lunch soon, and then he'll need a nap. While he's sleeping, I was hoping we could…talk about a few things."

"Talk?" The word came out in a squeak. He cleared his throat. "I mean, sure. That sounds like a good idea."

This was it. She was breaking up with him.

Breaking up? How was that even possible when they'd never officially declared themselves a couple?

And how many mixed messages could one woman give in the space of a few hours?

Before he could take a sip from the mug she'd handed him, his cell phone signaled a text. He pulled it from his hip pocket and read the message. It was Lila, telling him he could come over for the pie any time..

"I have an errand to run." He gingerly set his mug on the counter. "Shouldn't take more than twenty minutes."

Without waiting for a reply, he rushed to the front door, grabbing his jacket and truck keys on the way.

Maybe by the time he got back, he'd have figured out what he could say to keep her in his life as more—*much more*— than merely a friend and Tate's other grandparent.

Could things get any weirder between them?

Arms folded, Julia watched from the living room window as Lane's truck disappeared from view. And what sort of errand could be so urgent but required less than half an hour to complete?

Tate nudged his way between her and the window and peered over the sill. "Where Gampy go?"

"Good question. Want some lunch while we wait?" The sooner the little guy went upstairs for a nap, the sooner she could sit Lane down for their long-overdue heart-to-heart.

She found Tate's usual tortillas, hummus and sliced turkey in the fridge. He was swallowing his last sip of milk when she heard Lane coming in the front door.

"In the kitchen," she called.

He strode through the archway carrying what looked like a pie and set it on the counter.

Julia hiked a brow. "*That* was your errand?"

"Yep. Fresh from Lila Vernon's oven." He shrugged out of his jacket. Apparently, that was all he had to say on the subject.

Tate scrubbed the sleeve of his sweatshirt across his mouth. "Yay, pie!"

Using a dampened cloth, Julia cleaned the remnants of Tate's lunch from his fingers and face. "Nap time, fella."

Leaving Lane to deal with his pie and whatever else he had going on, she herded her grandson upstairs. He talked her into reading him one more story but fell asleep before she finished. After covering him with a blanket, she stepped away from the crib with a sigh. He was growing so fast. Another month or two, and he'd be ready for a toddler bed.

And where would *she* be in another month or two? Where did she *want* to be?

Time for that talk with Lane.

Enticing aromas—tomatoes and toasting bread?—drew her back to the kitchen. Lane stood at the stove, a wooden spoon in one hand and a spatula in the other. He shot a quick smile over his shoulder. "Didn't look like you'd eaten yet, and I'm starved. Hope tomato soup and grilled cheese sandwiches work for you."

Another stalling tactic? She shrugged. "I'll set the table."

They managed a few sentences of small talk over lunch. When Lane rose to wash dishes afterward, she stopped him. "Those can wait, can't they? I'd really like us to talk before Tate wakes up."

He nodded slowly. "Coffee first?"

Giving it a moment's thought, she said, "No, thanks."

"All right, then." Seeming to understand she was ready to get this conversation started, he gestured toward the living room.

They took opposite ends of the sofa, not too close, not too far apart, and angled slightly toward each other.

"If I did something—" Lane began.

"I've been wanting to tell you—" she said at the same time.

He lifted one hand. "Please. Say what you need to say."

She paused for a slow breath, her glance drifting toward the window. The snow was falling heavily now. If this conversation didn't go as hoped, she could be stuck here through an extremely uncomfortable weekend.

Directing a silent prayer heavenward, she marshaled her courage and faced him squarely. "The fact is, Lane, I think I'm in love with you, and I—"

He barked out a laugh. "You... You are?"

She flinched. "I don't see what's funny about it."

"No, I'm just relieved." Grinning, he shook his head. "I mean, considering how you left things this morning, I was afraid you were about to tell me the exact opposite."

Brow furrowed, she tried to recall what she'd said earlier. "It was only because..." Then her brain keyed in on a word he'd just used, and her pulse sped up. "Wait...you're *relieved*?"

"I am." He reached across the space between them to take her hand. His voice roughened as he said, "Because I've been trying for days to figure out how to let you know I'm falling for you, too. In a very big way. In fact," he went on with a nod toward the window, "since it looks like you'll be staying over tonight, you have every right to blame it on my prayers."

It was her turn to laugh. "You *prayed* we'd get snowed in?"

"Only if the conversation we're having right now went the way I hoped."

Warmth spread through her chest. "And did it?"

"So far...except for one small detail." Scooting closer, he drew her into his arms. With one hand cradling the back of her neck, he pressed his lips to hers in a kiss that erased any doubt whatsoever about his feelings...or her own.

When the kiss ended and she could breathe again, she snuggled against his chest. "I was worried you were still holding too tightly to your memories."

"Of Tessa? She'll always be a part of me. I can't change that. But she'd hate how I turned my back on life in a misguided effort to shield our daughter—and myself—from the world.

And I know she'd want me to be happy again." He kissed her forehead and hugged her closer. "To *love* again."

It would have been easy to rest there in his arms and dwell in the moment, but Julia hadn't yet shared everything on her heart. She gave his chest a pat and straightened but stayed close, her fingers weaving through his. "You should know why I reacted the way I did when you mentioned bringing the rocking chair to my house."

He stiffened slightly. "Okay…"

"It was because I don't know how much longer I want to live there."

"I don't understand. You want to move?"

"Lane." Heart ready to burst, she eased sideways to palm his cheek. "I want to make my home with you. Right here, where I've never felt more at peace."

He stared in disbelief. "But the clinic. Your work. How would you manage?"

Thoughts spinning, she realized the possibilities had been brewing in her subconscious since her first visit to the cabin. Abruptly, she rose and paced to the window. She returned to stand in front of him, but her gaze was fixed on the future. *Their* future.

Plopping down again, she clasped her hands between her knees. "I've been stressed and anxious for so long, believing that after my parents retired, the success of Frasier Veterinary Clinic would land solely on my shoulders. After Steven died, that burden only grew heavier, because he wouldn't be running the family business at my side."

Lane caressed her shoulder. "I can only imagine."

"Then, to learn it was only *my* dream, not his… It's changed my whole perspective." She sniffed back a tear. "We have two highly skilled doctors on board now, plus our excellent vet techs and a fantastic new office manager. The clinic has never run more efficiently."

"So…what are you saying?"

"I'm saying I'm ready to ease back, to take time for myself—for *us*." She cast him a watery gaze, her smile hopeful. "To create some new dreams with the man I love beyond imagining."

His lips skewed into a crooked smile. "Hmm, if you're contemplating spending most of your days…and nights…right here with me, we should probably make it official."

"That's what I was thinking." The look in his eyes sent warm tingles up her spine. She locked her fingers behind his neck, bringing them nose to nose. "Lane Bromley," she murmured, "will you marry me?"

His throaty chuckle tickled her face. "How does Monday work for you? Because that's the earliest we can get a license."

"Monday can't get here soon enough."

Epilogue

Five months later

Lane cast his gaze around Julia's kitchen—actually, Shannon's kitchen now. "Are you sure you have everything you need?"

"Yes, Dad, I'm sure. Thanks to you and Julia, there's plenty in the pantry and fridge to last until I get my first paycheck in two weeks."

"And your meds—you won't forget those, will you?"

"Dad. Stop fussing." His grinning daughter patted his cheek before setting another plate in the dishwasher. "I hear Tate waking up from his nap. Why don't you get him into his snowsuit and take him and Rowena out back to build a snowman? He's been begging to ever since he saw it snowed last night. By tomorrow, it'll all be gone, and I've been too busy settling in."

He shouldn't worry so much, but he couldn't help it. Shannon had been released from Mercy Cottage three weeks ago—praise God! She'd stayed with him and Julia at the cabin temporarily while reconnecting with "normal" life and with her little boy.

Yesterday, they'd moved her, Tate and the dog into Julia's house so she could be close to the new job she'd begin on Monday as part-time receptionist at Frasier Veterinary Clinic. Julia's mother had already volunteered—actually, she'd *demanded*—to watch Tate while Shannon was at work.

Later, watching his grandson pat mounds of wet snow into two lumps resembling a misshapen human and a legless dog, Lane's heart swelled with wonder and gratitude. How his life had changed in a matter of months! Yes, they'd experienced a few setbacks since Shannon had shown up at the cabin with her precious little boy, but he'd never been happier than he was at this moment.

Well, except for an unforgettable Monday evening five months ago when he and Julia had stood before Pastor Peters with their hours-old marriage license and pledged their love before God, Witt and Maddie, and the pastor and his wife.

The familiar rumble of Julia's SUV drew his attention to the driveway. Giving a wave, she climbed out and started through the side gate. After greeting Rowena with a scratch behind the ears, she sidled up next to Lane. "You guys look like you're having fun."

Grinning, he drew her into a one-armed hug while concealing the snow he'd scooped up with his other hand. "It's about to get a lot more fun."

"What— *Aaaagh!*" She yanked free, furiously brushing at the icy clump he'd shoved down the back of her collar. "You're in for it now, Gramps!" She grabbed a fistful of snow and aimed it at Lane's face.

He ducked just in time, but momentum sent him toppling sideways—right on top of Tate's snow figures.

"Gampy! Oh, no!"

"Oops. Sorry, Tater Tot." Lane scrambled onto his knees. "Grammy and I will help you fix them."

The back door opened and Shannon stepped onto the porch with her cell phone. Laughing, she snapped several photos while Lane and Julia attempted to rebuild Tate's masterpieces.

When they'd done all they could, Lane helped Julia to her feet. Studying their lopsided handiwork, he frowned. "Looks like we should keep our day jobs. Which reminds me." He planted a kiss on his wife's temple. "How'd your surgeries go today?"

"Both patients are recovering nicely. And in other news..." She turned to wrap both arms around his torso. "Dr. Kruger is ready to sign the partnership papers, *and* he has a colleague who's very interested in joining the practice."

Lane cast her a hopeful grin. "Does this mean you'll be cutting back on your hours even more?"

"I'd probably come in two days a week, just to keep an eye on things and stay in touch with my favorite patients."

"I can live with that...if you can." He studied her, wanting to be sure she wasn't hiding any reservations about the changes she'd been making. But all he saw were the eyes of love looking back at him.

And all he could do was lift his face heavenward in silent praise to God for giving him a grandson, for restoring his daughter, and—most especially—for filling his arms and heart with this bright, beautiful and utterly amazing woman.

It was well past sunset when Julia and Lane arrived back at the cabin. They'd have three whole days together before she'd head down the mountain again to see to things at the clinic. While he stoked the woodstove, she found some leftovers in the fridge to reheat for a light supper. While the food warmed, she brewed a pot of decaf for later.

With the dishes done, they carried their mugs to the living room, where Lane had positioned their rocking chairs facing the stove. As they sipped and rocked in companionable silence, with Daisy and Dash cuddled together on the plush bed near their feet, Julia savored the deepest peace she'd ever known.

She still couldn't quite believe they'd married so quickly, but neither of them had been willing to wait a moment longer to begin building a life together. Hadn't they both been lonely long enough? Their pastor, closest friends and Julia's parents had given their blessing as well.

And in this tranquil place, supported by her husband and dwelling in God's Word, she was coming to terms not only with the loss of her son, but with lost dreams as well. She'd always miss Steven, always regret the mistakes she'd made, but she was learning day by day to rest in God's forgiveness. Even more so, to forgive herself.

Lane reached for her hand. "Happy?"

"Incredibly." She glanced over at him, his features burnished by the fire's glow. "I thought the cabin might feel too quiet after the kids moved into my place. But now I'm more than ready for it to be just us."

"I miss them, but I'm happy for them." He drew her fingertips to his lips. "For *us*."

A tingle raced up her arm even as languid warmth spread through her limbs. "I know it's still early, but what if we let the dogs out once more and then head upstairs?"

He grinned. "That's the best suggestion I've heard all day."

* * * * *

Dear Reader,

Even as a confirmed introvert, I don't think I could handle living off the grid in the mountains. I'm too dependent on big-city conveniences—shopping, restaurants, medical care—not to mention reliable cellular and internet service. (Plus, I'm a warm-weather-loving Southern girl. Northerners are welcome to their snow and long winters!)

Sometimes, though, taking time away can be good, as long as it's for the right reasons. Prayer and contemplation can bring new perspectives about ourselves and our relationship with God. However, mountaintop experiences, whether literal or figurative, are intended to be temporary. Our purpose should be to return refreshed and restored, better equipped to face our everyday lives with grace and gratitude…or perhaps with deeper insights into any changes God may be calling us toward, along with the courage to take the next steps. I believe that's what Julia and Lane both discovered.

I hope you enjoyed coming along on this visit to beautiful Montana. I love hearing from my readers, so please contact me through my website, www.myrajohnson.com, where you can also subscribe to my e-newsletter. Or write to me c/o Love Inspired Books, 195 Broadway, 24th Floor, New York, NY 10007.

With prayers and gratitude,
Myra